The windshield seemed to explode

There was a single quiet snap that sprayed Plexiglas across them. Then a half dozen more rounds shattered the windshield.

"We're getting out!" yelled Fallon. He grabbed the collective and tried to jerk it up.

Rice leaned into it, holding it down. "Knock it off!" he shouted.

"Get us out of here!" Fallon screamed.

"Ayres, get him off the controls!" Rice was trying to keep Fallon from jerking the controls and flipping the aircraft. And then Ayres was there, an arm locked under Fallon's chin. Fallon lost his grip on the cyclic.

Rice checked the instruments. Everything was in the green. He pulled pitch. "Lead's on the go."

"You're off with four. One ship down in the LZ."

Rice wanted to beat the hell out of Fallon. It was bad enough having to sit in this Plexiglas world and let the enemy take potshots at him. He didn't need Fallon making it impossible

Also available by Eric Helm:

VIETNAM: GROUND ZERO
P.O.W.
UNCONFIRMED KILL
THE FALL OF CAMP A-555
SOLDIER'S MEDAL
THE KIT CARSON SCOUT
THE HOBO WOODS
GUIDELINES
THE VILLE
INCIDENT AT PLEI SOI
TET
THE IRON TRIANGLE
RED DUST
HAMLET
MOON CUSSER
DRAGON'S JAW
CAMBODIAN SANCTUARY
PAYBACK
MACV

THE RAID
SHIFTING FIRES
STRIKE

VIETNAM: GROUND ZERO™

TAN SON NHUT

ERIC HELM

A GOLD EAGLE BOOK FROM

WORLDWIDE®

TORONTO · NEW YORK · LONDON · PARIS
AMSTERDAM · STOCKHOLM · HAMBURG
ATHENS · MILAN · TOKYO · SYDNEY

First edition October 1989

ISBN 0-373-62720-3

VIETNAM: GROUND ZERO™

TAN SON NHUT

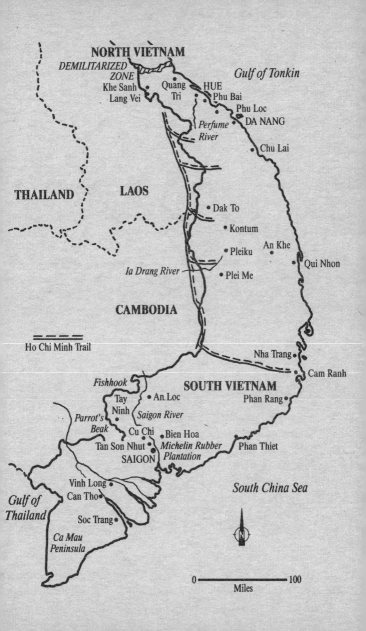

PROLOGUE

Pham Van Nhu lay in the thick vegetation south of the tiny village and listened to the night sounds. Quiet sounds that drifted on the light breeze, which did nothing to cut through the heat remaining from the day or the humidity that hung in the air. The air was so thick that it was almost impossible to breathe. It was so hot, even with the sun below the horizon, that the slightest movement caused him to sweat heavily. Already his black pajamas were soaked through. His hair hung in his eyes, and his palms were slippery with perspiration. He was afraid that his AK-47 might rust just from his touch.

Around him were the members of his twelve-man squad. They were a handpicked team who had come south together to be used as a weapon against the traitors who lived in South Vietnam. The men had been taught the tricks of guerrilla warfare as it was applied to the recalcitrant civilians. They knew ways to bend the thinking of the locals to that of the leaders of North Vietnam.

Like those with him, Nhu was a short thin man with a round face and dark brown eyes. His hair was jet black and straight.

Before leaving the North, the sides of his head had been shaved, leaving him with a shock of hair on the top of his head. The haircut was a trademark of the North Vietnamese Army. It distinguished him from the Vietcong. It meant that he was a real soldier and not a part-timer like most of the Vietcong.

Nhu and his companions had lain in wait since before dawn. They had filtered into the pocket of light jungle and heavy scrub that grew under the single canopy, staying there as the sun came up. They had remained motionless, the heat, baking the ground with the intensity of an oven, sapping their strength and creating a thirst that was almost impossible to ignore. They had watched villagers use the narrow path on their way to the rice paddies, the market or the other villages of the complex, never suspecting that North Vietnamese soldiers were close.

Nhu knew that a man could lie motionless in the jungle for hours while dozens of people walked by without spotting him. But the slightest movement would give him away. So he had to ignore his thirst during the day. He ignored his hunger and had tried to ignore the call of nature, but had failed. He used the trick that he had learned in the North and let his bladder go slowly so that the urine soaked the crotch of his black pajamas. There was nothing he could do about it, except try to control the flow so that there was no noise and no motion. He succeeded in that.

The day passed slowly. Nhu dozed slightly. He never fell completely asleep, always conscious of his surroundings. He was aware of the American helicopters overhead, of the distant booming of artillery and the occasional shouts of the farmers. When someone came close he snapped awake, but it was never their target.

At dusk, with the sunlight fading, he could begin to move, stretching his stiff and cramped muscles. Slowly he took out his canteen and sipped some water. He then inched it back down out of the way. He ate some of the cold rice from a small bag that he carried.

The foot traffic on the trail fell off. The farmers returned to their mud-and-thatch hootches and stayed there, fearing the night. The boys and girls slipped out to find one another in the dark so that the oldsters wouldn't see the games they now played, believing that they were the first to play the games. There was the noise of a radio somewhere playing the discordant music of South Vietnam broadcast by a Saigon station. A water buffalo bellowed in its pen. A single dog barked, was quiet for a few minutes and then barked again.

About midnight there was a rustling on the trail. A quiet, almost imperceptible sound as a single person walked along. Nhu turned his head and stared into the blackness. At first there was nothing to see except the shapes of the trees and the bushes that he'd spent the day memorizing so they wouldn't fool him after dark. But then against the charcoal of the jungle loomed another, darker shape. One that slowly took on human proportions.

As slowly as a man with arthritis, Nhu moved his hand toward the trigger of his weapon. He forced the thoughts of home and women and nights of pleasure from his mind as he studied the approaching shape. He touched the pistol grip of the AK-47, shifted it around and pushed the barrel toward the oncoming human.

For an instant Nhu wasn't sure what to do. They had known that the target was going to be walking along the trail late that night, but he couldn't identify the target. It could have been anyone. Someone innocent.

But then came the stuttering burst of an AK. A strobing light that flashed repeatedly, illuminating the surrounding trees and bushes. It was joined by another weapon and another until all twelve men were firing into the body that had fallen on the trail.

As quickly as it started, it ended. The noise seemed to echo for a moment, coming back at them a thousandfold. And then it was silent again. No more water buffalo bellowing, no more radio music and no more dog barking. The firing had ripped the soul out of the jungle and trampled it.

Slowly the men moved from their hiding places. They slipped up onto the trail and advanced on the almost shredded body of the dead man. The odor of fresh copper hung in the air, undercut by the stench of excrement.

Nhu looked down on the dead man. In the dimness of the jungle he couldn't see much. Blackness that was blood, and the gleaming of bone seen through holes in the skin, reflecting the harsh moonlight that filtered in through the trees. A dozen rounds, fifty, had slammed into the body, ripping it apart, exposing the internal organs and bone.

Nhu felt a tap on his shoulder and turned. One of his fellows signaled him and then slipped back into the jungle. Now they would begin the all-night task of fading away. Their job was done.

The headman of Luc Duc Four would be accepting no more aid from the Americans and the puppet soldiers of Saigon. He would be accepting no more aid from anyone. The message had been delivered, and those who found the body would know what it was. Now it was time to vanish as quickly as possible so that the villagers would not know how the job had been done. It would be one more chapter in the myth of the NVA. In the morning the villagers would find the body and know that working with the Americans and the South Vietnamese army would mean death.

The message was delivered and the lesson was over.

For now.

1

CONFERENCE ROOM
MILITARY ASSISTANCE
COMMAND, VIETNAM
SAIGON, RVN

The one thing that was constant in Vietnam was that the generals liked to be in air-conditioned surroundings. It made no difference that the soldiers were in the field, sweating in muck-filled rice paddies or living in rat-infested fire-support bases waiting for the VC and the NVA to swarm out of the jungle to kill them. The generals had air-conditioned trailers guarded by battalions of MPs. They worked in air-conditioned offices and conferred in air-conditioned conference rooms. It somehow seemed wrong.

Army Special Forces Captain MacKenzie K. Gerber, dressed in fresh jungle fatigues, the sleeves rolled to a point halfway between his elbow and shoulder as the current regulations prescribed, sat in the air-conditioned room, waiting for the briefing officer to condescend to put in an appearance.

Gerber was on his second tour of duty in Vietnam. On the first he had been in command of an A-Detachment at the old Camp A-555. This time he was assigned to MACV-SOG, which the news media was told meant Studies and Observations Group but which was the Special Operations Group. It was an umbrella that covered a multitude of sins. There was Project Phoenix, the systematic elimination of the Vietcong infrastructure; Blackjack, a guerrilla operation directed against the VC and NVA; and the Hard Rice drops of covert aid to Cambodians and Laotians who were fighting the Communists in their countries.

Gerber was a tall man, just over six feet. He had brown hair and blue eyes, and since his return to Vietnam, he had acquired a deep tropical tan. Although not stocky, he was deceptively strong. And although he was just over thirty, no one would quite believe it. Most guessed his age at twenty-five or on rare occasions, twenty-eight.

Next to Gerber was Master Sergeant Anthony B. Fetterman. If anyone could be described as deceptive, it was Fetterman. He was a short, thin, balding man with a heavy beard that required him to shave twice a day or look as if he hadn't shaved in two.

And even with that, Fetterman was the most dangerous man Gerber had ever met. He had catlike quickness and a ruthlessness that was necessary for the top-notch combat soldier. He could kill in an instant, like a cobra, with or without a weapon. He could slip through the jungle like a fog. And yet he was an educated, intelligent man who understood that fighting a war in the field was not the only duty of the soldier. He was also trying to learn as much about the Vietnamese people and their culture, turning that knowledge into weapons used against the enemy.

Fetterman leaned close to Gerber and whispered, "I could be at the hotel eating a good lunch."

"But the restaurant isn't air-conditioned," said Gerber.

"No, sir, but then I can stand a little heat if there's good food available. Besides, it's so cold in here it's downright uncomfortable."

"You've become acclimatized to Southeast Asia," said Gerber. "If you're a staff officer, they send you to Thule, Greenland before Saigon, just to get you ready for the air-conditioning."

"I think the American taxpayer would be upset to learn that he's footing the bill for generals who can't live with a little sweat."

"Do tell," responded Gerber. "The American taxpayer would be upset by a lot more than that if he knew what was going on over here."

"Yes, sir," said Fetterman.

The door at the far end of the room opened, and an officer in a khaki uniform appeared. It was a clean uniform, freshly pressed without a trace of sweat. Two rows of brightly colored ribbons decorated the left breast, along with a set of jump wings.

"Gentlemen, Brigadier General William Petrak."

Gerber and Fetterman, along with the other twelve officers and senior NCOs in the conference room, stood up to await the arrival of General Petrak.

The general swept into the room followed by three other men, two in jungle fatigues and one in khakis. Petrak moved to the head of the long and narrow conference table. As he sat down in the high-backed chair, one of the aides stuck a leather-bound notebook under his nose and then moved off. Petrak scanned it, flipped a couple of pages and then seemed to notice that everyone was still standing.

"Please be seated," he said, waving a hand.

Gerber sat down and studied his surroundings as he had done many times before. Nothing had changed. It was a typical military conference room. A slender table surrounded by chairs. There was a water pitcher in the center of it, but no water in it. The plywood walls were painted a sickly green and decorated with water colors done by local artists. Most of them were of jets at Tan Son Nhut, but a couple of them were street scenes, including one of an incredibly lovely Vietnamese girl of fourteen or fifteen.

The other people in the conference room were soldiers, all dressed in jungle fatigues. Some looked as if they had been in the field earlier; the uniforms were stained with mud and sweat-darkened, though the stains were shrinking under the influence of the air-conditioning.

"We'll get started if no one has any objections." Petrak didn't expect any. He glanced to the right and said to his aide, "If you'll proceed."

The man moved to the lectern stuck in one corner, pulled it out and then stood behind it. Satisfied with the positioning, he placed his own leather-bound notebook on it and then looked at the men.

"For those of you who don't know me, I am Captain Dwayne Leneer, assigned to the G-2 here at MACV." He let that sink in, as if he had let them in on something important. "Everything we discuss in this room is classified and will not be discussed outside of a secure facility or with individuals who are not cleared to hear it."

He stopped, letting them contemplate his words. Gerber shook his head. The man was a typical Saigon commando, figuring that everything he did and said was of supreme importance. But Leneer didn't have the look of a combat soldier. He was skinny and sunburned with Coke-bottle glasses over squinty eyes. His hairline had retreated, though he didn't look much older than thirty-five. If he hadn't been standing there in front of them in Vietnam, Gerber would have believed that he had escaped from a college classroom and that he wasn't a professor. Maybe a graduate assistant.

"Gentlemen," he said, staring down at them, "we've a problem building here." Again he stopped, as if for dramatic effect, but it might have been because he wasn't sure how to continue. The problem wasn't of extreme importance, in the scope of things, but it was an annoyance.

"Recently it has come to our attention that the enemy, meaning the North Vietnamese, has begun a ruthless campaign to win the hearts and minds of the South Vietnamese, and if that doesn't work, then to scare them into line with an orchestrated campaign of terror."

He slowly turned the page in his notebook. When he looked up at them again, he said, "Last night was the latest chapter in that campaign. An elder in the village of Luc Duc was murdered as he walked from his home toward a sister village. He was shot so many times that his family needed a sack to carry back his remains. The body was quite literally blown apart.

"Now," continued Leneer, "it was a politically motivated killing. The man was unarmed and was moving along an established trail. Apparently he had been marked for assassination because of his cooperation with our troops and his attempts to keep the enemy from using his village as a stronghold, recruiting center and supply depot."

Petrak looked at the young captain impatiently. "Thank you." As the captain left the lectern, Petrak continued. "What we've got here is a well-organized cell operating in the Boi Loi and Hobo Woods area. A small group, maybe a single man, but probably a squad."

"There a reason for believing that, General?" asked one of the officers.

Petrak turned and glared at the man, making it clear that he was not pleased with the interruption. But he answered the question anyway. "The physical evidence in the field. During their sweep, our people found evidence that seven or more men had been lying in ambush. That's based on the crushed vegetation and the expended brass found. Granted, the VC picked up most of their brass, but they left enough that we could put a comprehensive picture together."

Petrak glanced at his notebook. "What we've got is a terrorist squad roaming our area of operations, shooting anyone who talks to our soldiers. Any cooperation by the locals is almost the same as asking to be attacked. What we've got to do is field a number of quick reaction teams to find this squad and kill them.''

Gerber glanced at Fetterman and then looked toward the ceiling, as if searching for divine intervention. He knew what was coming and he didn't like it at all.

THE FIRST ROUND snapped through the windshield, scattering Plexiglas over both pilots. The aircraft commander couldn't duck because he was holding the controls. He could only sit there and hope that he didn't die in the next few minutes. Around him, M-60 door guns were hammering, and gunships were rolling in along the tree line, miniguns and rockets slamming into the enemy positions.

''Lead, you're down with ten,'' came the icy voice of the trail aircraft's pilot.

''Flight's taking fire on the left,'' said another voice calmly.

''Who's taking fire on the left?''

Warrant Officer John Newhawser ducked back then behind the metal plate by his head and tried to spot the new enemy threat. On the intercom he demanded, ''Jonesy, you see them? You got them in sight?''

The crew chief wasn't interested in looking for the enemy soldiers. He was busy firing his weapon into the trees, hoping that the M-60 rounds would keep the enemy from showing his face. Red tracers flashed out, hit the ground and bounced high.

''Chock four's taking fire on the left.''

''Lead, get out of there now!'' ordered the air mission commander.

''Lead's on the go.''

''Come off the LZ straight and stay low-level.''

''Roger, low-level.''

The lead aircraft lifted slightly, the skids dragging in the tall, dusty grass. The chopper raced for the tree line a hundred yards ahead of them. He was nose low, sucking in pitch, trying to get out before the enemy began to pour everything he had into the landing zone.

"Nine-six, this is Eight-one, we've got a thirty spotted in the trees."

"Lead, you're off with ten. Fire all over the fucking place."

"Can you hit it?"

"Roger, ten. Rolling over."

"Lead, proceed to the Papa Zulu and hold there for further instructions."

"Eight-one is rolling in . . . taking heavy fire." Behind that voice was the sound of machine-gun fire as the door guns shot it out with enemy soldiers on the ground.

"Roger, six."

"Lead, you're joined with ten."

"Roger, joined. Flight, come up a staggered trail."

Newhawser relaxed then, letting the tension drain from his arm and hand and then his whole body. He was suddenly out of the line of fire. Over the radio he could listen in as the gunships worked the tree lines so that the infantry could get off the LZ. Unless something terrible happened in the next few minutes, he wouldn't have to return to the hot environment. By the time the second lift went in, the enemy would either be so busy dealing with the grunts in the trees that they didn't have time to shoot at the helicopters, or they would all be dead and no threat at all.

Using the intercom, he told the peter pilot, "You've got it."

The peter pilot, Warrant Officer David Stockton, shifted in his seat and took the controls, one hand on the cyclic, one on the collective, and his feet on the antitorque pedals. He took a deep breath, as if he'd just entered the doctor's office and had been told to strip for a shot. Satisfied with his position, he said, "I've got it."

Newhawser released his grip on the cyclic and then sat back. He glanced over the rear of the armored seat into the mud-splattered cargo compartment and touched the floor-mike button with his foot. "How's everything back there?"

The crew chief, Spec Five Steve Jones, let go of the M-60 machine gun, and then looked around his side of the aircraft. There were no visible bullet holes and no indications that anything was leaking. He glanced around the transmission wall to where the door gunner sat and saw Marino hold up a thumb, telling him that all was well.

"We're fine back here, sir."

Newhawser nodded and then settled back. He glanced at the other aircraft in the formation, watching them as they seemed to bob up and down slightly. And even with the single bullet hole in the windshield, he felt good. They'd gotten in and out without anyone getting hurt. Thirty seconds of terror, neatly suppressed because he was flying the aircraft, because of his training, and then they were out of real danger.

"Lead needs a damage report from everyone. In chock order."

"Two negative."

"Three, several hits in the tail boom. All controls and instruments in the green."

"Three negative."

"Four negative."

Newhawser hit the floor button and said, "Five has at least one hit."

"How do you know?"

"Came through the windshield."

"Roger."

They continued on, with each aircraft reporting either nothing or a couple of minor bullet holes. Nothing that would knock any of the aircraft out of commission.

When they finished that, Lead announced, "We're heading back to the base. Officers' call at the club one hour after engine shut down."

"Now what in the hell does that mean?" asked Stockton over the intercom.

Newhawser grinned: "Means there is an officers' call at the club."

"But aren't we going back? We know where the enemy is and we're not going back?"

"No need for us to go back. Grunts can take care of the situation without us. The men on the ground, with gun support, are sufficient to take care of the VC. Obviously someone has decided that it's not necessary for us to stand by, so we've been released for the day."

Newhawser leaned back and put one foot up on the instrument panel and thought about the mission. For a kid almost fresh from high school, he hadn't done too badly. There had been a year of flight school between graduation and his orders for Vietnam, but now his tour was winding down, with no more than eighty-two days left before he was on his way home to the land of the big PX and the all-night generator.

Like most of the pilots, like most of the soldiers fighting in Vietnam, Newhawser was young. Nineteen years old, with a high school education and above-average intelligence, which somehow hadn't been enough to keep him out of the Army. After a year in Vietnam, he was underweight by twenty pounds. He had long brown hair, blue eyes and an angular face that was tanned a deep, dark brown. The bones of his face were sharp, and if he went without sleep for twenty-four hours, he took on the features of a human skull. It was a frightening transition.

Stockton wasn't much different, except that he'd only been in Vietnam for three months. He had yet to lose the last of his Stateside fat and hadn't spent nights in a bunker waiting for a mortar round or rocket to fall on him, ending his short life abruptly. He was still caught up in the myth of the great military adventure and believed in the cause for which they were fighting. If asked, he wouldn't have been able to articulate the cause, other than to say that they were trying to defeat Communist aggression in Southeast Asia.

It could be claimed that Newhawser and Stockton were brothers. They were nearly the same height, just a shade under six feet. Although Stockton's hair was darker and shorter, he had the same blue eyes. Those who didn't know, suspected they were related. They were two of a kind. Peas in a pod. And neither had seen the other until Stockton arrived in Vietnam.

"You want it?" asked Stockton.

"Nope. You keep it. You need the practice, and I don't feel like flying anymore."

In the distance he could see the oval-shaped base camp that was Cu Chi. On one side of it rose a column of thick white smoke. It had always been there. From the first day that Newhawser had flown as the greenest peter pilot to the day he took his AC checkride, to that afternoon, the column of smoke was there. Once he'd thought it was because of construction on that side of the base, but now he knew that construction wasn't the answer. It was some kind of a dump or landfill where they burned everything before covering it over, probably to deny it to the VC and the locals.

He reached down to the radio and flipped the switch up. The ADF was tuned to AFVN, and although he didn't like having it on in the background during the combat assaults, he didn't mind a little music as they were heading home. Rock and roll that was six months out of date.

"Flight, come up trail."

The formation shifted slightly, one aircraft falling in behind the one in front of it and slightly above, to stay out of the rotor wash. When they had finished, Trail announced, "Lead, you're in trail."

"Roger, trail."

They began a slight turn, approached from the north and landed on the open field to the west of POL. Once they were down, the flight splintered, each of the helicopters hovering toward one of the refueling points. Newhawser grinned as Stockton struggled to land. The rotor wash from the other choppers caught him and bounced him around, lifting and dropping the skids as if he was still a trainee at Fort Wolters. He tried to stabilize the hover, failed and finally, in frustration, shoved the collective down, dropping the aircraft to the pad.

"Christ, take it easy," said Newhawser, trying not to laugh. "You'll spread the skids and I'll get blamed for it."

Jones hopped out of the cargo compartment and walked around the nose of the aircraft so that he could help Marino with the refueling.

As they did, Newhawser leaned to the right and plucked the book from the map case at the end of the console. As he began to fill out the paperwork, he said, "Looks like we get to red X this sucker."

"Why?"

With the end of his pen he pointed at the bullet hole in the windshield. "That makes it a red X. Can't fly it until maintenance gets it fixed."

Finished, he stuffed the book back into the slot. During the night a clerk would move through the nest, collecting the top sheets in each book in each aircraft so that he could log it all onto master forms. These would be sent to battalion, then to group and probably brigade. Someone else would look at all the information and design a series of papers and reports that would be compiled into a useless file for transmission to the Pentagon.

Jones and Marino finished the refueling and climbed into the cargo compartment. As they did, Trail reported, "Lead, looks like everyone is refueled and ready."

"Roger." There was a moment of silence as the lead pilot called the tower to arrange for a quick flight from POL to the nest. When he received the clearance, he radioed, "Lead's on the go."

One by one the helicopters took off, stringing out behind the lead aircraft. The formation never joined. It stayed low over the perimeter wire and then slipped along the active runway, slowly descending until they were hovering along the nest. Each then peeled off, maneuvering toward the revetments.

Newhawser sat back as Stockton parked the aircraft. He slipped it into the sandbagged barricade, sticking the nose up against the short wall. The rotor wash swept the interior, churning a cloud of dust and paper up through the rotors and then back down. Hovering there, Stockton pushed the collective down slowly and this time, without all the turbulence created by the other nine helicopters, he was able to land the chopper gently.

They ran through the shutdown procedure and sat waiting for the rotor to stop spinning. When it did, Newhawser climbed from the cockpit and took off his flight helmet. He waited for Stockton and they climbed into the back of the truck that drove up to ferry them from the nest across the runway and to operations. They checked in there, turned in the SOI, the survival radio, and filled out the last of the paperwork.

As they climbed the operations bunker stairs and stepped onto the boardwalk, Newhawser said, "I'm heading over to the club so that you can buy me a beer."

"What the hell for?"

"Letting you ride with me today. That has to be worth at least one beer."

Stockton shook his head in disbelief. "But you made me do all the work."

"Of course. That's the job of the peter pilot. You do all the work and I get all the credit."

Stockton gestured toward the club and said, "Then by all means let me buy you that beer."

They walked past the orderly room and the company offices, past an open field that separated the enlisted men quarters from the officer hootches. They arrived at the officers' club, a long low, white building with a corrugated tin roof, no windows and a wall of sandbags about four feet high around the outer wall.

They entered the side door and moved to the right where they hung up their helmets and pistol belts. As Newhawser walked toward the wicker chairs and tables, Stockton moved to the bar where he ordered the two beers and paid for them with the MPC they used instead of greenbacks.

The club had a huge open floor that was sometimes filled with tables and chairs, and sometimes open for dancing, whenever they could entice the nurses from the Twelve Evac Hospital to come down for a visit. There was a stage in one corner that was brightly lighted. Arrayed along one wall were slot machines that used tokens, which could be bought from the bartender. Two huge fans stood near the open doors creating a roar but not much of a breeze.

Slowly the rest of the officers filtered in. Each stopped by the bar for a beer or two, or a can of barbecued potato chips. After a few minutes, Company Commander Major Howard Devane strolled in. He waved off the bartender and walked to the stage. He stood there for a moment, hands on his hips, wearing jungle fatigues that looked starched and tailored. He'd be considered an old man for Vietnam, nearly thirty-five. He had short black hair, a round suntanned face and fine features.

"Gentlemen," he said finally. When no one paid any attention to him, he said it again, louder. Slowly the noise of conversation faded until the only sound in the club was the roaring of the fans. Devane looked at one of them and a captain leaped to turn it off.

Newhawser whispered to Stockton, "I don't think I like the looks of this."

One of the other officers behind Newhawser leaned forward and tapped him on the shoulder. "Last time this happened," he said, "we ended up moving from Pho Loi to Cu Chi."

"Shit," said Newhawser, "and I had the decorator scheduled for next Tuesday."

"Gentlemen," said Devane, "let's get down to business so we can go over to the mess hall before they run out of food…"

"How would you know if they had food? I've never seen any there," asked one of the warrant officers lost in anonymity in the back of the room. There was a bark of laughter in response.

Devane shrugged. "I need five volunteer crews. Five ACs and five peter pilots. Might be a week, ten days, or it might be for a month."

Silence descended on the room. No one looked up at Devane, afraid he'd interpret the stare as an assent. There was a single cough.

"Gentlemen," said Devane, "if I don't get the volunteers, I'll have to make the assignments. I don't want to do that because it just isn't fair."

The captain who had jumped up to turn off the fan finally raised a hand. "I'll go, sir."

Now Devane shook his head. "No, I'm going to need you here if we come up with the five crews that we need to send to Saigon."

He said it quickly, almost as if trying to slide over it without the pilots hearing it. But that didn't work. Everyone caught the words and realized it was a mission that would be staged from Tan Son Nhut, putting them close to Saigon where there were things other than 16 mm prints of movies they'd all seen before being shipped to Vietnam. There were women in Saigon, round-eyed women who weren't outnumbered by the men.

Almost as if an order had been given, the men were on their feet volunteering for the unknown duty in Saigon.

"Well, thank you all," said Devane, grinning broadly. "I knew I could count on you. The names of the lucky few will be posted on the scheduling board by nineteen hundred tonight. Questions?"

There were none.

2

THE WIRE SERVICE
BUREAU SAIGON

Robin Morrow sat at her desk in the city room, staring off into space. In the weeks and months since the Tet offensive, she had moved toward the front row where she could see out the windows along the wall. A bank of windows ran from one side of the room to the other, allowing the journalists to look out across the street to another building that mirrored the one in which the wire service bureau was housed. Sometimes there would be something interesting to see. Several times it had been a naked Vietnamese woman, sweat glistening on her body, dancing to some unheard music. Morrow had found that uninteresting, except the one time the woman had been joined by a naked man and the two of them attempted to make it standing up. Then Morrow had stood at the window cheering him on, just as her male counterparts had cheered the woman.

The city room was filled with old beat-up desks, many of them salvaged from MACV when the army bought new equipment. Most of them were painted battleship gray, though a few had been personalized with salvaged paint, the colors ranging from a light green to a hideous blue. Each of them had a typewriter, again a mixed bag, some of them old Underwoods or Royals, and only a few of them electric IBMs. The problem was that the power was so unreliable that the IBMs were often worthless except as expensive paperweights.

Along the back wall was a row of file cabinets that were supposed to contain information about any subject the reporters could want to write about. But they weren't used much since the clerk who maintained the files had been wounded during Tet. No one else had the patience or the desire to do the job. Not when a simple phone call could get the information in half the time with half the work.

A row of glass-enclosed offices used by the editors and a few of the top-ranked correspondents occupied another wall. Morrow had yet to work her way to an office, though there was a glass cubicle she could use if she felt the need for a little privacy. She shared that with a dozen others, and it was on a first-come-first-served basis.

Morrow was a good-looking woman, tall and slender with brown hair bleached blond by the tropical sun. Her hair was cut in bangs that brushed her bright green eyes. She wore her standard uniform, a khaki jumpsuit with the legs cut off at mid-thigh, the sleeves chopped off and rolled above her elbows, and the zipper pulled partway down.

Finally, bored with sitting there and staring at nothing, she got up and walked over to one of the editors' offices. She tried not to think about the letter that had come from her sister, Karen. Although it held nothing designed to irritate her, it had done that.

She saw Mark Hodges sitting behind his miniature desk, feet up, cigarette smoke curling above the newspaper he held in front of his face. She tapped on the door.

Hodges dropped the paper to his lap and looked up at her. He was a short, overweight man with black hair he had greased down so that the comb marks were still fresh in it. Unlike the majority of the people in Saigon, he did not have a tan. His skin was a chalky white, the result of a conscious effort not to go outside during the day. He hated the tropics, the humidity and Saigon. He hated everything about his job, except that he was in charge. That he loved.

"What can I do for you?" he asked Morrow.

She stepped into the office and tried not to breathe too deeply. The air was bluish, filled with the smoke from the cigarettes he'd started chain-smoking.

"That's a good question," she said. She stood there, looking at the soles of his shoes, worn thin with holes at the balls of his feet. The last thing she wanted to tell him was that she was out of ideas and that nothing was coming to her. She knew the source of the irritation but worked to keep it suppressed. She was bored enough to finally admit it, and hoped he could suggest something.

Hodges grinned at the news and dropped his feet to the floor. "I've a couple of things."

"Why don't you give me one?"

Hodges nodded and shifted through the stuff that cluttered the top of his desk. He sorted it into a couple of piles. Taking the cigarette from his mouth, he said, "I've got an interview scheduled with the embassy about the civic action programs being conducted by American civilians who are working with the South Vietnamese military."

"Pass."

Hodges crushed out his cigarette. "Yeah, I didn't think it sounded very good." He found another sheet of paper. "How about the nurses assigned to the various evac hospitals? What's it like to be a woman in a combat zone?"

"Pass."

"That'd be a good one," said Hodges.

"Not for me." She folded her arms across her chest. "I'm sure they're doing a hell of a job under circumstances that are less than adequate, but it's not a story for me."

Hodges nodded and flipped through a couple stacks of paper. "New general assigned to MACV. Guy named Petrak. I think he was promoted just before he arrived in-country."

"Christ," said Morrow. "That's all they need over here. Another general who doesn't know what the fuck he's doing."

Hodges stared up at her. "You know that your language has really gone to hell in the past few months."

"So who cares?"

Hodges raised his eyebrows. "You are in a bad mood. Want to tell Uncle Mark all about it?"

"Shut the fuck up."

He waved a hand at her. "Come on in and shut the door."

She dropped into the tattered chair reserved for visitors. It was a cloth thing that once had been green, but the sun had faded it and red dust had covered it, turning it into a muddy crimson with only hints of the green showing through. She leaned back and crossed her legs.

"Now," said Hodges, "what's really going on?"

"What do you mean?"

"I know you, Robin. You're not the type to sit around and wait for a story to come to you. You go out and find one even if you have to arrange it slightly. You don't like to be handed a second-rate story."

"So what's your point?"

Hodges picked up his cigarettes and opened them. He shook one out, held the pack up to her and waited for her refusal. Then he lighted it and sat back. "The point is, you're not the type to sit around. So something is wrong."

"I appreciate your concern," she said, "but it's nothing that won't be fixed in a few hours or a couple of days and a stiff drink."

Hodges smoked quietly for a moment and then said, "If you are really looking for a story, I've got something here about the murder of a village elder or chief or whatever the hell they call them. You interested?"

She held out a hand. "Sure. I'll look into it, but I can tell you right now that it'll turn into another nonstory. Vietnamese official murdered by other Vietnamese. No one's going to give a shit about it."

"Well," said Hodges pushing a sheet of paper at her, "look into it until something better comes along."

She stood up and grabbed the paper. "Sure." She moved to the door and said, "I'm leaving for the day."

"Fine. Go."

She did.

WHEN THE MEETING ENDED and Gerber had been handed his assignment sheet, he was unhappy. The whole thing seemed to be ridiculous. But he took the sheet anyway and got the hell out before he said something to the general that would come back to haunt him later.

Outside, standing at the edge of the huge parking lot that was filled with jeeps, trucks and only a couple of staff cars, Gerber shook his head again. "Never going to work."

"No, sir," agreed Fetterman. "But it gives the paper pushers something to think about." He walked past two posts with the white-painted chain that separated the parking lot from the rest of the MACV grounds.

Gerber followed Fetterman to the jeep and climbed into the passenger's side, after tipping the seats to the sitting position. They had tilted the seats forward so they wouldn't bake under the tropical sun. Fetterman unlocked the steering wheel, dropping the chain and padlock to the floor of the jeep.

"Where to now?"

Gerber glanced at the paper again. He wiped his forehead on the sleeve of his jungle fatigues. The contrast between the air-conditioning of the conference room and the outside was startling. In one place it was cold enough to be uncomfortable, and in the other hot enough to be miserable. The sweat had blossomed on his body during the short walk to the jeep, soaking his jungle jacket, turning the green material black under his arms and down his back.

"I look at this," said Gerber, "and can't see a thing on it that suggests we need to begin anything this evening. Tomorrow morning we're scheduled to be over at the SOG building at Tan Son Nhut. We can organize our strike force there. Helicopters are being coordinated by Army Aviation and the Intel work is being done through the G-2."

Fetterman nodded. "Might be a good idea to give Kepler a call. See if he knows anything that could help."

Gerber put a foot up on the dashboard. "Maybe pull a few strings and have him assigned to us."

Fetterman started the jeep and drove to the entrance of the parking lot. "Downtown or Tan Son Nhut?"

"Downtown. Probably be our last night in the hotel. Tomorrow we're going to have to stay out at the SOG building with everyone else."

Fetterman nodded and entered the traffic, turning onto the main road. He fell in behind a deuce and a half, slowing down so that the truck could pull ahead of him. Clouds of diesel smoke poured from it, settling toward the rear.

"Can't get used to it," said Gerber. He saw the puzzled look on Fetterman's face. "The bureaucrats who end up in positions of power and begin to try things that the last group tried. We end up doing the same things over and over."

Fetterman negotiated a turn and then asked, "Why didn't you say something?"

Now Gerber laughed. "Oh, come on, Tony. A general is not going to listen to a captain. You know that. Or rather he'll listen and then say in the best managerial voice, 'Let's try it my way this once.' I think every one of them has taken courses in effective corporate management, and there isn't a leader in the bunch."

Fetterman stopped for a line of pedestrians crossing the street. Office workers, men and women, American and Vietnamese, who were fleeing from their jobs and heading to the bars of downtown Saigon. A tall Vietnamese woman with long, jet black hair seemed to float in front of him.

Then he turned his attention back to the captain. "You have to roll with the punches."

"Christ, Tony," snapped Gerber, "this whole idea is asinine. We'll be tying up assets that could be more effectively employed elsewhere because some minor Vietnamese official got himself killed."

Gerber's gaze wandered to the people on the streets as he tried to figure out why he was suddenly in such a lousy mood. Maybe it was the ineptitude of the people running the war. With almost everyone's tour lasting only a year, there was no real continuity. Things that had been tried last year were being tried this year because no one remembered they had failed. One man could get a good feel for what needed to be done in his AO, and then he rotated home and with luck, never returned to Vietnam. Everything he learned was lost.

Now they were seeing it again. A brand-new general sent in with his brand-new ideas. Except they weren't new. They were old and useless.

They began to move again, drifting along with the traffic made up of lambrettas, old cars that had been painted a hundred different colors, military trucks and civilian buses. There were bicycles and pedicabs. A swirling mass of people all trying to forget the war for a few minutes as they searched for some type of human contact.

"I think my problem," said Gerber, "is that I've suddenly grown too old for this shit."

"I'm older than you, Captain."

"Yes you are," said Gerber. He wanted to say something more about that, but didn't know what it would be.

"And everyone is too old for this shit, but it's the only war we've got."

"I never thought I'd hear you say something like that, Tony."

Fetterman laughed. "Neither did I. But it's true. Besides, you've got to remember that we're both just little cogs in the great MACV war machine."

"I think you've hit it there, Tony. It's the frustration of knowing what to do, but not being allowed to do it. There's always someone who outranks you with what he thinks is a better idea. I know the idea sucks, and you know it, but he's a general so we have to go along with it."

They slowed and stopped again. Fetterman wiped the sweat from his face with his hand, rubbing it on the thigh of his jungle pants. "The one thing we do know is that the plan isn't so poorly designed that people are going to get killed by it."

"And, there's the possibility that something might come of it, even by accident."

They started again and turned down a wide street. Fetterman saw a parking place and slipped across two lanes to claim it. There was a blare of horns from angry drivers behind him. He ignored them; courtesy went out the window in Saigon.

"You know," said Gerber, "if you leave the jeep here, it'll be gone by morning."

"Yes, sir. But I'm going to call the motor pool and have them pick it up. Then tomorrow I'll get another one. Now, what's the plan for the evening?"

"That's a very good question. I don't have a plan. At least not yet."

"Then, if I might suggest," said Fetterman, "let's get cleaned up and have a good meal here. Tomorrow we might be eating C-rations or worse."

"Can't think of anything worse," said Gerber, "but I understand. I'll meet you in the lobby in an hour or so."

NEWHAWSER, ALONG WITH every other pilot, was in the operations bunker waiting for the list of names to be posted. The

CO hadn't told them much more about the mission, other than they would be on standby at Tan Son Nhut, and that had been enough. Saigon was the lure, and every one of them rose to it.

As soon as the meeting had broken up, some of the officers had gone to see Major Devane, hoping to convince him that they should be assigned to Saigon. Others had gone to their platoon leaders with similar arguments. Those who were the cleverest went to see the operations officer, hoping that he would put in a good word for them. And those who were pessimistic pretended they didn't care one way or the other, figuring that indifference was the best ploy.

None of that really worked. Devane saw it as an opportunity to get rid of the officers he believed were troublemakers. He selected those men whose military bearing was not the best. He was going to get rid of the men who wore their hair too long, had tailored their fatigues too much, who complained too frequently or who questioned the war and its various leaders. A general housecleaning to improve the unit.

When the list was posted, Newhawser found his name at the top. Stockton was also on it, as was Chester Cramer and Don Logan. Newhawser grinned when he saw that. It meant that the party would begin on landing and continue until they had to return to Cu Chi.

The only thing wrong with the list of people chosen was Captain Paul Fallon. He was a new officer, assigned in the last month, who had just completed his in-country checkride and his CA checkride but had yet to fly a real combat assault mission. Such a man might not believe in all-night parties, chasing women, both round-eyed and Vietnamese, and might not fully appreciate the pressure felt by young men in war.

Fallon was a very tall, thin man who looked almost emaciated. He had short black hair and a single eyebrow over both his bright blue eyes. His features were sharp and his face bony. His ears looked like jug handles.

Newhawser slapped Stockton on the shoulder and nearly shouted, "Looks like they've stuck all us bad apples into one barrel. Except for Fallon."

The operations officer watched the men for a moment and then said, "Takeoff is scheduled in thirty minutes. We're ferrying the aircraft to Tan Son Nhut tonight."

There was a cheer from several of the men.

"Captain Fallon, if you'll come with me, I'll get you briefed on the mission and the expectations. You have a choice for your AC?"

Fallon, who had been standing in the rear of the crowd, shouldered his way forward, glanced at the list of names. "Mr. Rice would be fine."

The operations officer surveyed the crowd and yelled, "Rice, you here?"

"Christ! Why me?" said a voice in the rear.

The operations officer ignored the question. "I would suggest the rest of you get your gear together and get out to the nest. Aircraft assignments will be posted in fifteen minutes."

Newhawser turned and walked up the stairs and stepped out. He stopped and sat on the wall of sandbags that protected part of the bunker. He watched as the others trooped by, but didn't feel inclined to join them.

Stockton appeared and asked, "What are you waiting for?"

"What's the rush? I pick up my weapon, flight helmet and throw some fatigues into a duffel bag. Five minutes and I'm ready to go."

"So why are you sitting here?"

"Just thinking." He turned and faced the younger officer. "You notice that everyone on the list would be considered a screw up?"

"So?"

"So, nothing." He grinned. "Most of those on the list are the best pilots. They don't conform to the lifer's way of thinking, but they're all good pilots. Looks like Devane is stripping the heart out of the company so that he can turn it into a model of military precision.''

Stockton shook his head. "I don't understand."

"Man, a military unit does not operate by the book and succeed. The book gives you the basics, but to make a military unit, it has to have a soul. It can be built in by an effective leader, or it can grow with men who have fought together, but it has to have one. Devane has just stripped the soul from this unit. He's trying to kill it."

"But we'll be in Saigon . . ."

"Not forever. Four, five weeks we'll be back. But this isn't going to be the company we left." He shook his head slowly and glanced to the flight line and the nest. "Too many managers in the Army now and not enough leaders. The few they have, they shift around, trying to find a slot for them."

He stopped talking and suddenly grinned broadly. "Or a better way to look at it is that they've taken the soul of the company and put us all together. Hell, we'll become the best damn aviation unit this United States of America Army has ever seen. The absolute best."

He hopped off the wall. "I guess it's now time to pack. See you here in ten minutes."

"Okay."

Newhawser felt like running suddenly. Excitement bubbled through him. He wanted to scream. Instead he forced himself to walk calmly toward his room and tried not to think of alcohol-soaked nights in Saigon. The last few days of his tour weren't going to be all that bad.

3

CAN ME TO REPUBLIC OF VIETNAM

The VC squad had slipped through the jungle for most of the day, rested during the heat of the afternoon and then finished the journey as the sun set. It had been a long, hot journey, made worse by the buzzing of American helicopters and the roar of American jets. Aircraft hovering around clearings and rice fields like birds of prey waiting for something to expose itself.

When the helicopters disappeared, the squad began moving again, ever so slowly, listening for the sounds of enemy soldiers. The pace, however, was steady. A creeping movement through the jungle avoiding the trails and paths worn by both humans and animals. They slipped around giant trees, under bushes and down to the edge of small streams, walking carefully so that they didn't leave a trail for the Americans to find and follow. The desire was to be no more disruptive than an early-morning fog.

When they stopped in the afternoon, they ate a hasty lunch of cold rice. They dropped none of it and left nothing behind to show anyone where they had been. Finally, with the heat dissipating and darkness falling, they began the final leg of the journey. Just before it was completely dark, they found themselves at the edge of the jungle, no more than a hundred yards from the mud-and-thatch hootches of Can Me To.

They spread out, taking cover in the deep grass at the edge of the jungle. The village was spread out in front of them like a toy town. There were a couple of cooking fires, and two lanterns provided a little light. At the far end was a cinder-block-and-tin structure that was the school building. It was a gift from the Americans. And along with the school-teacher and the headman, it was the target.

Nhu anchored one side of the line, watching the dirt road to the east and the first few hootches in the village. A woman, hunched with age, walked from a cooking fire to the door of a hootch and stopped there. She turned, seemed to look right at him, and then disappeared inside.

As they watched and waited, the sun vanished, wrapping the ground in a velvety darkness. Activity in the village slowed and then almost stopped. The sky overhead was free of Americans.

The squad leader, Nguyen Lam Van, stood up and walked to the very edge of the jungle. Someone in the village, if looking, could have seen him and shouted a warning, but no one was looking.

Van waved a hand, and the others stood up and formed a line. They moved forward in the direction of the village. At first no one saw them. They were phantoms from another war.

Then one of the villagers, standing in the open door of his hootch, spotted them. He stared, his mouth open, not wanting to shout because that would call attention to himself.

Nhu and the rest of his squad moved through the center of Can Me To until they reached the schoolhouse. It was a single-story building with a bell in front, constructed of material supplied by the American Special Forces and built by the villagers with the help of the Americans.

Van pointed to it, a symbol of the cooperation between the Americans and the locals. "I want it destroyed."

While Nhu stood guard, four members of the squad disappeared inside. There were sounds of wood breaking and of blackboards being smashed. Two of the desks flew out the door and landed on their sides. A third joined them and then the men reappeared.

"It is ready," said one of them.

Van pushed the three desks together and then stomped on them, breaking them into smaller pieces. When he had a pile of rubble, he stooped and scraped together a pile of splinters. Using an American-made lighter, he set the rubble on fire and then stood back, letting the flames build.

Nhu watched as one by one the villagers left their hootches and came to the center of the hamlet. They stood in the shadows, just outside the flickering light of the flames, watching as the remains of the desks burned.

"It's time," said Van. He walked over to the bell and began ringing it. The noise seemed to echo through the village, picking up strength. It was unnaturally loud.

But it worked. Those who hadn't been drawn out by the destruction in the school came out now. A hundred of them standing in a semicircle, close enough to see what was happening but far enough away to flee if they decided that was the intelligent thing to do.

Van turned and faced the villagers. He held his AK high so that they would be sure to see it. The weapon had become a symbol of the VC and the NVA. The Communists carried it while the puppet soldiers of Saigon and the American invaders from across the ocean carried the M-16.

"You have been duped by the puppets in Saigon," Van shouted. "They have seduced you with stories of wealth, promises of gold, and lies of freedom. They have come to your village to corrupt the young and kill the old. They bring presents and tell you they want nothing in return."

He pointed at the school. "They tell you they want to teach you the things that will make you free, and then fill your heads with lies. They want only to suppress you and enslave you, and the first step is to pretend to educate you."

Van and his men moved toward the crowd. One of the men crouched on the ground and lighted a fuse. It sputtered and began to burn.

At the sight of the sparks, the villagers shrank back. Van and his men walked away from the school and tried to find shelter behind the mud hootches. They watched the villagers who seemed mesmerized by the burning fuse.

There was a rumbling from the interior of the building and then an explosion. Fire boiled up, lifting the roof and shredding it. The walls seemed to bow out and then broke apart, collapsing to the ground. Dust rolled out and up. A couple of women screamed, but no one moved.

"You see?" said Van, his voice rising. "You see? It is nothing now."

He walked over and kicked the post that held the bell. It would have been dramatic if the post had fallen over, but that didn't happen. The bell rang and the post vibrated, but it didn't fall.

Van spun and stared at the people, dark shapes hidden in the shadows.

"Where is the school-teacher?"

No one answered.

He moved toward them and pulled back the bolt of his AK, ejecting a round. The metallic noise of the machined parts sent a shiver through the crowd. He lowered the barrel of the weapon, pointing it at the belly of the closest male. Van grinned at him but didn't pull the trigger.

"The school-teacher?"

The man shrugged helplessly. "I . . ."

Van whirled, facing the whole group. "Do you people want this man to die for no reason? We will kill him unless you demonstrate that you have seen the error of your ways. Where is the school-teacher?''

A slight young woman pushed herself out of the shadows and moved forward. ''I am the teacher.''

Van nodded slowly and turned so that his AK was now pointed at her belly. ''What do you teach them?''

She shrugged. A slight movement of her shoulders. ''Vietnamese history, English, how to read and to write.''

''Why English?'' demanded Van.

''Because our country is filled with men and women who speak English.''

''No,'' said Van. ''You will not teach the children the language of the imperialist swine. You will teach them nothing about the Americans.''

She didn't respond.

Van waved a hand, gesturing at the ruined school. ''You see what happens when you cooperate with the Americans. We want nothing from them, except to be left alone.''

The teacher stood with her head bowed, as if she were examining the ground at her feet. The villagers had moved away from her, afraid that she was somehow going to infect them. They wanted nothing to do with her now that she had been singled out by the NVA officer.

Van stepped closer and put the muzzle of his weapon against her belly. With his left hand he reached out and lifted her chin, staring at her round delicate face, masked by the shadows and the darkness around them.

''Lessons are taught and soon forgotten,'' said Van quietly. ''Warnings are given and ignored. Unless there is a demonstration to reinforce the lessons and the warnings, they are quickly forgotten.''

Her eyes grew wide with fear. Her lips trembled but she didn't speak. She tried to look away, but Van held on to her chin, his fingers squeezing tighter and tighter, but she refused to cry out.

"Defiance," said Van, "cannot be tolerated. We are in a war here, and those who do not support us are our enemies." He looked beyond her to the villagers cowering in the shadows. "Punishment is the answer."

There was a moment of complete silence and then a single shot. The sound was muffled because of the proximity of the body. The teacher groaned as she was thrown back. She hit the ground in a sitting position, then slowly toppled to the side. As she fell, she wrapped her hands around her stomach and moaned quietly.

One of the men took a step forward but Van swung his rifle barrel at the man. Nhu, who had been in the shadows watching, moved forward. The Vietnamese farmer stopped.

Van began lecturing the villagers. "You see what happens to those who fail to listen. You see what happens to those who refuse to understand our position."

He turned and pointed at the smoking ruins of the school building. "Those who defy us will be eliminated. Those who support us will be rewarded."

For a moment he stood there, trying to stare into the eyes of each villager. The moaning of the teacher was fading as she lost more blood and slowly died. When she was finally still, Van waved at his men.

"We go now," he told the villagers. "But we'll be watching. If you cooperate with the Americans or their puppets from Saigon, we will return. The punishment will be much more severe the next time."

Two of the soldiers broke away from the group, moving toward the jungle. One by one the others followed until only Nhu and Van were left standing in the village. Nhu turned and ran into the jungle. Van was right behind him.

FALLON TOUCHED THE floor-mike button with the toe of his boot. "Lead's on the go."

Rice held the controls. He had turned ninety degrees to the right and looked along the side of the active runway at the four other aircraft lined up there. Satisfied that each of the ACs was ready, he turned again and faced the wind. Lowering the nose slightly, he raced forward and then pulled back on the cyclic as he sucked in more pitch. They began a rapid climb over the Three Quarter Cav hangar, passed the long, low, sandbagged quonset huts of the Twelfth Evac Hospital and then the southern perimeter wire. Just beyond it was the silver ribbon of Highway One.

They crossed to the south side of the highway and turned to the east. Rice leveled off at fifteen hundred feet and held the airspeed to sixty knots.

"Lead, you're off with five and joined."

"Roger. Rolling over."

Now Rice increased the airspeed to eighty knots. He glanced to the right where Fallon sat, a map on his lap.

"You don't need that. We follow the highway for a while, then descend under the approach paths to Tan Son Nhut and pop up to land at Hotel Three."

"Fine," said Fallon.

Rice laughed, knowing that the captain would not be able to hear him. The roar from the turbine and the constant popping of the rotor blades made normal conversation impossible. That was the reason for the intercom system.

Rice grabbed the cyclic in his left hand and reached over to the radio control head. He hit the "NAV" switch, which was tuned in to AFVN. Rock and roll filled his earphones. The crew chief had turned it up when no one was looking. Rice turned it down so that he could hear the other radios over the music and then sat back, taking the cyclic in his right hand again.

"To the south," said Rice, "is a swamp. We rarely get out over it. Beyond that is the Oriental River. There's a couple of Special Forces camps there we support."

"Okay," said Fallon.

Rice shot him a glance. He was aware of the strange situation that now existed. Technically, while the aircraft was airborne, Rice, a warrant officer, was in command. Captain Fallon had to take orders from him. But Fallon was the mission commander, which meant he was in command of all the aircraft. Rice had to take orders from him. Fallon didn't have the time in-country or the hours in a Huey to be assigned as an aircraft commander and therefore had to fly with a pilot who had AC orders. Rice in charge again.

And the rules were not those set up by the company, but were in effect countrywide. Pilots with less than three hundred hours of flight time were not given AC orders. They had to get the experience and then be approved by the other ACs.

Rice decided to take a shot. "You know, you're going to have to learn the landmarks and the company procedures before they turn you loose with an aircraft."

"But I don't need a wobbly one to give me the instructions," snapped Fallon.

Rice took a deep breath and then switched both his intercom and Fallon's to the PVT setting. It meant they could talk to each other without the crew chief or door gunner listening in.

"There's something that we need to get straight right now," said Rice.

"Sir," added Fallon.

"I don't think so," said Rice. "Not while we're airborne or aboard this aircraft."

"I'm the mission commander," said Fallon.

"And I'm the AC. You can't take off without me. In matters concerning this aircraft, my word is final."

"I outrank you," said Fallon.

"Not on this aircraft you don't. You'd better understand that now. I will do my job the best way I can. That includes teaching you the things that you didn't learn in flight school and that you'll need to survive in-country.''

Outside he saw the golden glow of Saigon. Bright lights that attracted Americans, Vietnamese and Charlie's rockets. Tan Son Nhut was on the western side of the city.

Rice squeezed the mike. ''Beginning the letdown.''

''Mr. Rice,'' said Fallon, ''I don't care for your attitude, and I'm going to report it to Major Devane as soon as we land and I can make contact with the company.''

''Go right ahead,'' mimicked Rice. ''Get me in trouble and have me sent home for a court-martial. See if I care.''

''You're a smart ass, aren't you?''

''Makes no difference, Fallon,'' said Rice. ''You call the major and tell him that I was trying to instruct you on the AO and the procedures but you were so busy being Captain Fallon that you wouldn't listen. Devane will have your ass for breakfast.''

''You're awfully sure of yourself.''

''It's happened before, Captain,'' said Rice. He aimed at a break in the trees that was half a mile wide. Rather than hug the ground as he would have done during the day, he stayed at fifty feet. The light from Saigon, the moon and the stars made it easy to see the obstructions in front of him.

Fallon didn't want to let it drop. ''I'm reporting this to the major,'' he said again.

''How we doing back there, Trail?'' asked Rice using the radio.

''You're still joined.''

''Roger. Coming up now.'' He glanced to the right and left and then said, ''Contact Hotel Three, number four on the preset, and tell them we're a flight of five needing to touch down there temporarily. They'll tell you that we can't shut down, but you say we have orders to do just that.''

Fallon said, ''Preset four.'' He hesitated, then added, ''We'll be taking this up later.''

"I'd let it drop," said Rice. "You'll just get your ass in trouble for not listening to me."

Fallon started to say something and then changed his mind. Instead he asked, "Preset four?"

"Right. Give them our tail number and that you're a flight of five."

Fallon tuned the frequency into the UHF and then flipped his switch to the number-two position. Using the floor-mike button, he said, "Hotel Three, Hornet seven six seven inbound with a flight of five."

"No," said Rice. He reached over and flipped his radio around and made the call again, telling Hotel Three that they were south of the field with a flight of five for Hotel Three.

"Roger, Hornet seven six seven." The tower cleared them for landing, gave the current winds, other traffic and then the altimeter setting. "You're cleared to land."

Rice said, "Easier than I thought."

They entered the traffic pattern and landed, coming in low over the corrugated tin roof of the World's Largest PX. Rice shot the approach long and toward the right, aware of the four aircraft that were behind him. Once they were down, he turned and waited as the other helicopters maneuvered backward toward the chain-link fences that separated Hotel Three from the rest of Tan Son Nhut.

Once everyone had parked, Rice keyed his mike. "Shut them down."

"Refueling?"

"We'll have to take care of that in the morning, either on the airfield or back at Cu Chi."

Rice then started through the shutdown procedure. As he did, he saw a man run from the terminal set off to the left and under the control tower for Hotel Three. Rice stripped his flight helmet and opened the cockpit door.

The man ducked low under the rapidly slowing rotor blades, stepped up on the skid and said, "You can't shut down here."

Rice stared at him, glanced right and left and then said innocently, "But I already have."

"No, sir. You have to start up and get out."

"We're here for the night," said Rice.

Fallon leaned over and asked, "Is there a problem?"

The man saw Fallon's captain's bars. "Sir, local regulations prohibit the shutdown of nonpriority aircraft on the Hotel Three facility."

"Mr. Rice?"

Rice took that to mean he was to handle the situation. He wiped his face and then replied, "We've orders for here. Until we learn exactly where we're to stand by, we'll stay right here. Now you can go wake your airfield commander, get him over here and then we'll drop a few names. He'll find he's acted rashly, we're to stay and you'll look like a jerk. Or, you could cut us some slack and no one gets into trouble."

The man stood there silently for a moment. Rice was so sure of himself that the man didn't know what to do. Finally he asked, "How long you going to be here?"

"Overnight at the worst. We'll be off here and to our new assignment in the morning."

"Well, sir, I guess it'll be okay. Where will you be staying?"

Rice looked at Fallon. The captain shrugged. "We'll be working out of SOG."

"All right, sir. But you'll have to move the aircraft in the morning."

"No problem," said Rice. He reached up and shut off the rest of the switches as the man retreated toward the terminal.

One of the other aircraft commanders, Lee Hoskinson, strolled up. He leaned against the side of the chopper. "What's the deal now?"

"I don't know, Lee," said Rice. "What's the deal now, Captain?"

"I suppose to coordinate with the SOG people. You know where that is?"

"Over on Tan Son Nhut proper," said Rice. "Check in at the terminal and they'll get you a ride over there. Meantime me and the rest of the boys will be in the club."

"What about the enlisted pukes?" asked Hoskinson.

"They'll have to stay with the aircraft," said Fallon.

Rice shrugged. "They can hit the EM club."

"Mr. Rice," said Fallon.

"Look, sir, you can't leave them out here. If they're at the club, we'll know where they are and can find them. Nothing's going to happen tonight, anyway."

Fallon sat quietly for a moment and then said, "All right. The club and nowhere else. They can return here if they want. Sleep in the back of the helicopters."

Hoskinson said, "Maybe you'd better go with the captain and make sure we get everything we need."

Before Fallon could speak, Rice cut him off. "Come on, Lee, the captain will be able to get us quarters, check on the refueling situation and get us the maps of the local area. He knows that much."

"Okay."

Rice unbuckled his seat belt and threw the shoulder harness over the back of the seat. He climbed out of the helicopter and then walked around to the nose so that he could open the access panel there. He'd thrown his baseball cap in when he'd made the preflight.

"You going to postflight it?" asked Fallon as he climbed out.

"That's your job as the peter pilot."

"I'm supposed to be over at the SOG building."

Rice shrugged. "War is hell. I'll be at the club."

Rice walked over to where the other four aircraft commanders stood. Together the group walked off, figuring that if anyone wanted them, they could find them in the club.

As they reached the gate leading off Hotel Three, Hoskinson asked, "How'd it go with Fallon?"

"Man's an asshole. Thinks because he's a captain, he knows it all. We might be in trouble with him."

"So what're you going to do?" asked Newhawser.

"Drink," said Rice.

4

THE CARASEL HOTEL
SAIGON

Gerber sat with his back to the door, wishing he'd taken the other chair, because having his back to the door bothered him greatly. He told himself that such concerns were foolish, and the fact that Wild Bill Hickok had died with his back to the door in Deadwood, South Dakota had no meaning for Gerber in Saigon, South Vietnam. Besides, Fetterman could see the door, and long before anyone could ambush him, Fetterman would either warn him or eliminate the problem.

They had ordered a big dinner, figuring that it would be the last opportunity for a decent meal for a while. It was true they'd be at Tan Son Nhut, but they might find themselves in the field for a week or more with almost no warning. Because of that, they decided to stuff themselves.

They sat in the plushest restaurant in the hotel. It was alive with light from the crystal chandeliers. There was flocked red paper on the walls, floor-to-ceiling windows that looked out on downtown Saigon, tables with red cloths and white linen napkins and the finest silverware. Crystal glasses and fine china adorned the tables. It was one of the last restaurants in Saigon that could boast of an elegance that had been the norm in Saigon before the war. The one with the Americans, the one with the French and the one with the Japanese.

It was a restaurant that was marked with contrasts. The elegance inside and the obvious war outside. In the sky above Saigon were parachute flares. Brightly glowing lights with smoky trails above them, slowly descending, brightening the darkest of the corners.

Fetterman sat there with a slight grin on his face and the remains of his meal scattered in front of him. He had demolished the appetizer, which had been a shrimp dish with a tangy red sauce, salad covered with a French dressing, the vegetable and the meat, and had even called for dessert. Now, sipping his coffee, he looked contented. He'd found a ticket to the rich life that was only glimpsed at by civilians who could scarcely afford tickets to the movies.

Gerber wasn't quite as happy as Fetterman, but he had eaten everything in sight just as Fetterman had, and now drank the last of the wine. He was sweating slightly from the effort of eating so much, but didn't mind. The air-conditioning was laboring to cool him.

Fetterman set his coffee cup down and looked right at Gerber. "You have a date tonight?"

"Nope," said Gerber shaking his head. "Robin said something about working late."

"Not anymore." He nodded toward the door.

Gerber turned and saw Morrow standing there. She wore a light dress in pale green. It hugged her body with a skirt that ended above the knee. Her hair had been brushed, and hung to her shoulders.

"You going to invite her over?"

Gerber stood up and waved. Morrow saw him and then started toward them. As she approached she said, "I thought I'd find you two here."

"Why?" asked Gerber. He pulled out a chair for her.

She sat down, pulled a napkin off the table, snapping it open. "Because you two are always eating in the best places when you have nothing else to do." She fell silent for a moment and added, "Or just before you head out on some kind of mission."

"Tonight it's a case of having nothing else to do," said Gerber.

She indicated the debris on the table. "You've finished eating already."

"But if you're hungry, we'll stay here and watch. Maybe Sergeant Fetterman could eat another dessert."

"Maybe some coffee," she said.

"There something wrong, Robin?" asked Gerber.

"I don't know," she said. "I just feel out of sorts, you know? Like something's about to happen but I don't know what it is."

"Impending doom?" asked Fetterman.

Morrow shrugged. "I don't know. I feel something bad is going to happen. It's like those feelings in school. The big test is coming, you know it's coming and you're unprepared for it. Same feeling."

Gerber plucked his napkin from his lap and wiped his lips. "There's only one treatment for that sort of thing."

"A good fuck," she said.

"I don't talk like that," said Gerber. "And besides, I was thinking of a drink. A good strong drink."

"I'll take it," she said.

Fetterman cleared his throat and pushed back his chair. "I think I'll just head on over to the SOG building and see if anything's happening there."

Gerber wanted to protest but couldn't. Anything he said would be misinterpreted by Morrow. As a reporter, she would be interested in anything happening at the SOG that was scheduled. To protect the mission, Gerber had to pretend that nothing was happening there.

"Don't volunteer us for anything, Tony," he said.

Fetterman grinned. "I wouldn't do a thing like that. You know me."

Gerber looked at Morrow. "By tomorrow he'll have us in a plane ready to jump into the middle of a VC stronghold."

"There any of those left?" asked Morrow.

"To my knowledge," said Fetterman, "the Vietcong have ceased to exist as an effective fighting force. The Tet offensive destroyed them."

"There you have it," said Gerber.

Fetterman hesitated, waiting for Gerber to mention the bill, but when he didn't, Fetterman walked away.

"Alone at last," said Gerber.

"Don't joke around," she said.

"Something bothering you that I should know about?" asked Gerber.

"No." She sipped at the coffee that he had poured for her from the carafe on the table. "I just don't know. It seems that, oh hell, I don't know. Maybe it's just that I've been here for so long and nothing changes."

"Then go home," said Gerber.

She looked up at him sharply. "That what you want?"

"No," he said, "but it might be what you need. Hell, even the Army is smart enough to limit the tours of the soldiers here. One year in Vietnam, one year in the World. The only exceptions are those who volunteer for more time in-country, and even then they get a month back in the World."

"But that's for the men fighting the war."

"Hell, Robin, we're all fighting the war in one way or another. You've seen more action than most of the combat officers I know. That's got to be taking a toll. I think you deserve a rest Stateside."

"You're just trying to get rid of me."

"Not at all." Gerber leaned closer to her. "But everyone needs a rest. This place gets to you after a while."

"It get to you?"

Gerber nodded slightly. "It gets to everyone. That's why you have soldiers drinking themselves into oblivion on passes. For a few hours it helps to forget what has gone on or what will happen. I'm surprised that more people over here don't crack up."

She looked around the restaurant. At the soldiers in poorly fitting civilian clothes with Vietnamese women who were earning a living by being with them. There were diplomats with young American secretaries, and officers from the various commands in Saigon dining together. There were a few American nurses from the local hospitals. The point was that everyone in the room was involved in the war in some fashion.

"Can we get out of here?" she asked.

"As soon as I get the check."

"Fetterman kind of dodged out of here leaving you stuck with it."

"Not really," said Gerber. "He bought the last time we had a big meal, and he did give me a chance to say something. I figured I owed him some food."

Almost as if he had been listening for a cue, the waiter swooped in and asked, "Was everything satisfactory?"

Gerber said, "It was fine. The check?"

The waiter gave it to him and then left them alone.

"I'm not spoiling your evening, am I?" asked Morrow.

"Hell, Robin, I would have called you if you hadn't told me that you had something else on for tonight." Gerber stood and sorted through the MPCs issued by the Army. He calculated the tip carefully, remembering Fetterman's constant reminders that overtipping, along with paying inflated prices, did not help the locals. He dropped the money on the table. "Where would you like to go now?"

"You have any Beam's?"

"Always."

"Then I'd like to go to your room and drink as much of it as I can before I pass out."

They left the restaurant and walked across the marble lobby. Thick columns supported an ornate ceiling two floors above them. Gerber ignored the people sitting on the furniture scattered around the lobby, the clerks behind the teak-and-mahogany desk, and headed straight for the elevator. They entered it and rode up to Gerber's floor.

They walked down the hallway and even the dim lighting did nothing to hide the threadbare, stained carpeting. There were narrow tables spread out along the walls. Some held lamps that created pools of light, and others held vases or flowers. There were paintings of local scenes.

Gerber unlocked his door and shoved it open. Morrow stepped in, turning on the light as she did. She then moved toward the bed and sat on the edge.

"Bottle's in the wardrobe," said Gerber, searching for a glass in the bathroom.

"Locked," she said.

Gerber returned and handed her the glass. He stopped long enough to punch at the air conditioner built into the wall just under the grimy window that looked out on downtown Saigon. In fact, the whole room seemed to be an afterthought. The air conditioner added after the hotel was built, the wardrobe against the wall, stuck in there because there was no closet space. There was a chair that didn't match the rest of the decor, and a ceiling fan that turned slowly but did little to cool the room. The carpeting, like that in the hall, was old, stained and might once have been tan.

Gerber unlocked the wardrobe, which contained his uniforms, underwear and another set of civilian clothes. At the bottom was his duffel bag, a bandolier of M-16 ammo, his rifle and a Browning M-35 pistol. Next to his spare boots was the bottle of Beam's. He'd opened it the day before and had only taken a single drink.

Morrow held out her glass. "Pour."

Gerber filled her glass and then sat down in the chair. He kicked off his low quarters and leaned back, taking a long pull at the bottle. "That's smooth."

"Very," said Morrow. She drank half the glass in a single hasty gulp that brought tears to her eyes.

"Take it easy," warned Gerber.

"I'll take it any way I can get it," she said. She held out the glass and Gerber filled it again.

"You sure there isn't something else going on?"

She slipped to the rear, sliding up the bed until she sat on the pillow, her back against the wall. She crossed her legs, saw that her skirt was hiked up and ignored it.

"Nothing's wrong," she said. "What could possibly be wrong?"

"Your sister has gotten orders for Vietnam," said Gerber.

"Karen resigned her commission and is working in a hospital in Nevada. Desert Springs or Desert Hope or some damn dumb thing. She's found a doctor, loaded, and the two of them are going to get married and live happily ever after, with more money than either of them deserves."

"Ah," said Gerber, suddenly understanding. The rivalry between the Morrow sisters was coming to a head. Karen, the favored one, who had gone into nursing as a career to help people, had just snagged the brass ring. Or in this case, the gold ring. Complete with diamond.

Robin, the sister who always trailed behind, who had gone into journalism, who was spending more time in Vietnam than most combat soldiers, was growing old with no prospects for the future. The Morrow grandchildren would be a product of Karen and the sign of another failure for Robin.

"Ah?" she said finally. "What in the hell does 'ah' mean?"

"It means I think I now understand."

She took another healthy slug of whiskey and held out her glass for more. Gerber moved to the bed and filled her glass again.

"You'd better slow down on that stuff. Drink it too fast and you don't get drunk. You get sick."

"Can't even drink right," said Robin quietly.

Gerber shook his head. The smart thing was to get out now. If he stayed, she'd continue to drink and her mood would turn black. When she was drunk and upset, there was no telling what she might do. Once, to embarrass Gerber, or maybe just to get his attention, she had stripped in a bar to the excited cheers of a hundred GIs. She'd danced on a bar wearing only her see-through bikini panties.

"You're drinking just fine," said Gerber. "Did you have dinner?"

"You never called for dinner."

"Not my fault," said Gerber. "I thought you had an interview or something tonight."

"Nope. Went away."

Gerber leaned over and set the bottle on the floor. He turned slightly and looked at Robin. In the half-light from the dim bulb supplied by the hotel, she was prettier than ever, even for a drunk.

"Let me ask you something," said Gerber. "You happy with what you're doing?"

She held up the glass. "You mean drinking?"

"You know what I mean," said Gerber.

She took a swallow and then faced him. "Happy?" She shrugged.

"I mean," said Gerber, "do you like your job? Are you happy with your life?"

"Yeah, I guess."

"Then who in the hell cares what your sister is doing or going to do. Want to bet that she's happy? And if she is now, how about in six months? We both know what kind of person she is. She's a predator, and the kill doesn't do a thing for her. It's the hunt that she thrives on.''

''What's your point?'' asked Morrow.

Gerber reached over and took the glass out of her hand. He took a drink and said, ''It's this. Don't worry about Karen. She has style and she has grace, but she doesn't have substance. You do.''

''She's getting married.''

''That what you want?'' asked Gerber.

''You asking me to marry you?'' asked Morrow.

Now Gerber laughed. ''Word games. No, I'm not asking you to marry me. I'm asking you if you want a marriage just to get married. Live in the suburbs, have half a dozen kids and go to the PTA.''

''Anything wrong with that?''

''No. If that's what you want.''

She shook her head. ''I don't know what I want. I just feel that it's all passing me by. I sit here, surrounded by a half million American men and I can't stand them.''

''Thank you,'' said Gerber.

''You know what I mean. Except for you and Fetterman and a couple of others, the majority of them seem like idiots. Like you said—no substance. The best years of my life are right now, and I'm not getting anywhere with them.''

''Robin, you're not powerless. You can make a decision and take control of your life.''

She was silent for a minute, maybe longer. Finally, in a quiet voice, she asked, ''Is there a chance for us?''

Gerber knew that a flip answer, quick and insincere, was not the right response. She had suddenly bared her soul to him, and if he didn't treat the question with the respect it deserved, then the whole relationship would crash and burn. If he was tired of her, this was his chance to be rid of her.

But that wasn't what he wanted. He stared at her, thought about the question and wished she hadn't posed it then. He would have liked to have waited to answer it. The confrontation came too quickly.

"A chance for us?" repeated Gerber. "Of course there is." There was more to say, but he didn't know how to say it. Not without seeming to be condescending.

"That's all I ask," said Morrow.

Whatever else he might have said was interrupted by a knock at the door. As Gerber stood, she leaned over and retrieved her glass of whiskey.

Gerber stepped to the door and shouted through it, "Who's there?"

"Sergeant Fetterman, Captain."

Gerber opened it. "This had better be damned important."

Fetterman nodded, looked beyond him at Robin Morrow sipping her drink. "It is. They've struck again."

Gerber knew immediately what Fetterman was talking about. He groaned quietly. "Let me get changed and I'll be right with you."

"Yes, sir."

NEWHAWSER, ALONG WITH Lee Hoskinson, Sam Rice, Dean Spilman and John Cruz, also known as Juan, had been sitting at a table minding their own business for most of the night. Newhawser had bought the first round of drinks and they had finished them quickly. They got a second, drank it, then began singing along with the jukebox that was stuffed into the corner of the officers' club.

They were sitting in the main club area, a huge room dominated by a bar along one wall. It was a massive dark thing with rows and rows of liquor bottles stacked behind it, and tended by a dozen or so people. The floor space was crammed with tables, with the exception of a small wooden square in front of the slightly raised stage where a band played periodically. The band had abandoned their instruments and were now at the bar.

The place was jammed, mainly with pilots who had finished the day's work and were now trying to forget all about it. There were a few people in civilian clothes, some of them workers from the American embassy and a few contract workers for various civilian companies. The few women were badly outnumbered, and most of them were looking to make some extra money later in the evening.

Newhawser and the other pilots didn't care about any of that. They were on assignment in Saigon, away from the strict control of Major Devane. Unlike the majority of the others in the club, they were teenagers—with the exception of Rice, who had turned twenty a few months earlier. In a sane world, they would have been freshmen and sophomores in college, unable to legally buy alcohol. In Vietnam they were senior pilots, aircraft commanders who were responsible for a quarter of a million dollars' worth of aircraft and the lives of three others. Those who flew lead could multiply that by ten.

But with no one watching who knew them, they were like the kids whose parents were gone for the evening, leaving them alone for the first time. Nothing was off-limits. By the third round they were getting wild.

Rice finally stood up, climbed onto his chair and looked over the crowd. He was weaving slightly as he held his glass high and announced, "I need a woman." He pointed at one of the Vietnamese girls in a short skirt and a sweat-damp blouse. "You. I need you. Now. Beaucoup bucks."

She glanced at the fighter pilot she had been talking to and then stood up, waving at Rice.

"Yes," he shouted over the din of voices and the music of the jukebox. "Come to me. I need you now."

Another Air Force pilot stepped close, looked at the assembled warrant officers and said, "You better get your friend down and shut him up."

"Why?" asked Newhawser. "He needs a woman."

"You are officers and gentlemen, and this sort of action is not proper."

Rice tried to turn, nearly fell and then righted himself. "Officers, yes. Gentlemen, no."

"Why don't you Army pilots grow up?" yelled another Air Force officer.

"Why don't you Air Force pilots come down and fly in the war?" snapped Rice. With that he leaped at the first officer who had spoken, knocking him to the floor.

"Oh shit," yelled Newhawser as he stood up quickly, knocking over his chair.

The pilot who shouted moved forward, a fist cocked. Newhawser intercepted him, spun him and hit him on the side of the face. Pain flared in his hand as the man grunted in surprise and stumbled to the rear.

"Fight!" yelled Cruz. "Fight!"

Rice turned and caught a punch in the cheek. He staggered back and then attacked. He struck an Air Force pilot twice. As the man retreated, Rice grabbed a bottle.

Hoskinson kicked back his chair and grabbed the shoulder of an Air Force pilot and shoved. The man fell to the floor. Another pilot threw a punch but Hoskinson ducked, kicking the man in the knee.

Spilman joined the fray, slamming a fist into the face of a pilot. The man collapsed, spitting blood. He looked surprised that anyone would hit him.

"All right!" yelled Spilman.

As quickly as it started, it ended. The Air Force pilots and everyone else backed off, forming a circle around the Army pilots. Both groups stood staring at one another for a moment. Newhawser dropped into his chair, cradling his sore hand. Cruz grabbed a drink and downed it.

And Rice, who had started it, climbed back to the chair and demanded, "Bring the victor a wench." He wavered back and forth as if he were about to fall.

There was a sudden commotion near the entrance as Air Police, carrying billy clubs, and with .45s on their hips, entered the club. The leader moved right to the bar. One of the men there pointed toward the Army pilots in the center of the crowd.

Newhawser looked stricken. "Oh-oh."

"We can take them," said Rice, recklessly.

"Sure," agreed Cruz, "but do we want to try?"

Newhawser picked up what was left of his drink and held it high. "To the Hornets!" he shouted, then downed his drink.

The others did the same.

The officer in charge of the Air Police approached and stood in front of Newhawser. He slapped his club into the open palm of his left hand menacingly. "You coming along peacefully, or you going to make it difficult?"

For a moment Newhawser thought about it. Then he shrugged and said, "We're through."

"Then come along with me."

Newhawser turned toward the others. "Let's go, boys."

They followed the Air Police lieutenant across the floor and then out the door. The trip to Saigon hadn't started out all that well.

5

SOG BUILDING TAN SON NHUT

They left the jeep parked outside the single-story building that was the SOG Headquarters. Fetterman didn't bother to lock the vehicle, figuring there was no one awake to steal it. Not to mention the fact that none of the Special Forces men would steal a vehicle from a fellow SFer.

Fetterman opened the front door and stood back, letting Gerber enter first. They entered a narrow hallway made of bare plywood, now covered and stained by the red dust of South Vietnam. To the right was a dayroom complete with a small black-and-white television, a radio tuned to AFVN, a beat-up record player and a small refrigerator. There was a single table with four chairs around it, a couch upholstered in green cloth, a couple of mismatched chairs, and end tables covered with old magazines.

They continued down the hall and entered the briefing room. In the center was a long table for reading maps. There were chairs around it, again mismatched, more maps on the wall, and a wall locker filled with grease pencils, pens, rulers and dozens of other office supplies.

Two Special Forces troopers sat waiting. Derek Kepler, the Intelligence sergeant that Gerber had used on his A-Detachment during their first tour, acknowledged Gerber and Fetterman. Kepler was a large man with dark hair, a tropical tan and a new puckered scar on the side of his face.

Next to him was another sergeant Gerber didn't recognize. He was a lean young man with thick black hair, light, sun-burned skin and small, almost delicate features. He didn't look as if he could withstand a strong wind.

When Gerber and Fetterman entered, Kepler grinned broadly. He stood and held out a hand. "Captain Gerber, good to see you again, sir." He nodded at Fetterman. "Tony, how've you been?"

Gerber shook Kepler's hand. "Good to see you, Derek. You been keeping out of trouble?"

"Yes, sir. Haven't stolen a thing in a couple of months. Makes my hands itch."

"The jeep outside," said Fetterman, "the one right out there, is mine."

"I wouldn't take anything that belonged to you," said Kepler.

"Who's your friend?" asked Gerber.

"That's Sergeant Richard Hansen. He's over from MACV and has charts and graphs and all kinds of interesting things for us to look at. And he brought us some brand-new Intelligence about that assassination squad."

Gerber pulled out a chair and sat down. Leaning forward, he said, "Let's get to it."

Hansen took a map, spun it around and pointed at a small village that was northwest of Cu Chi and almost due south of Nui Ba Den.

"This is Can Me To, part of a five-village complex that has been friendly to the South Vietnamese government and to us for several years. We've built a school there, run regular civic actions programs such as the introduction of sanitation and medical treatment. One of your Green Beret doctors gets in there once or twice a week to treat the infections and minor cuts and bruises.''

"Understood," said Gerber.

"There are almost no booby traps in there. Farmers find them and remove them. Other places, the farmers know where they are and leave them alone so that we trip them. Here, they take them all out."

"Friendlies," said Fetterman.

"Very," said Hansen. "Tonight they were hit. The VC put a squad into the village, destroyed the school and then murdered the teacher. Shot her in front of the villagers. All this happened little more than two hours ago."

"How'd we get this so fast?"

Hansen turned and nodded at Kepler. "Network of agents in there, sir. Number of them I trained back when we had the old Triple Nickle. One of them radioed the information back to us as soon as the VC were gone."

"Two hours," said Gerber. "Quite a head start for the enemy. Wouldn't do us any good heading out there now."

"No, sir," agreed Kepler. "As soon as they shot the teacher, they got out. Warned the locals not to cooperate with the Americans or the South Vietnamese anymore and then they got the hell out."

"So, even if we had the assets standing by, wouldn't do us any good."

"Damn," said Fetterman. "Tomorrow, we'd have had the choppers and the strikers on station to do something about the attack."

"Which reminds me," said Kepler. "There's a Captain Fallon here who is the pilot in charge of the helicopters."

"They've arrived?" asked Gerber.

"Yes, sir."

"There anyone around here who could hit the field in an hour? Fifteen, twenty men?"

"I think I could scare up that many," said Kepler. "Hell, with you, me and Tony, we've got three already. You want to meet this Fallon?"

"Of course."

Kepler stood and said, "He's in the back."

Gerber and Fetterman followed Kepler. They moved down a hallway and into the back room. It was a small room with a cot against one plywood wall, an old wooden chair and Fallon sitting there like a prisoner in a cell.

"Captain Fallon?"

The young officer looked up. He glanced at Gerber, then Fetterman and back at Gerber. "Yes, I'm Fallon."

"Gerber. Special Forces. I understand you're the flight leader here."

Fallon stood and moved to shake hands. "Five aircraft and crews. Few things to work out yet. Logistics and the like, but we're ready to go."

"In an hour?" asked Gerber.

"Well . . ."

"Captain," said Gerber, "we've got a fix on the target now, and if we get airborne, we might be able to end this thing by dawn."

Fallon looked sick. He rubbed his face with his fingers. There was a quiet rasping of skin against beard.

"Right now, I'm afraid my crews are scattered all over the base. I'm not sure where they are."

"An officer should know where his men are at all times. Especially in Vietnam. Especially because the situation can change so quickly."

"We were told that nothing would be required of us until tomorrow morning. We were to get here this evening, find quarters and be prepared to fly tomorrow after meeting with you for a briefing here."

Gerber shook his head and glanced at Kepler. "Derek, sounds like you don't have to find the men tonight after all."

"It's not my fault," said Fallon.

Gerber looked at him. "I want you ready to take off by zero eight hundred tomorrow morning. All five ships."

"Yes, sir."

"Derek, I'll want twenty-five men to go with us. Straight legs if nothing else is available, but I'd prefer to have some of our own people."

"You're not going to find twenty-five SFers unassigned around here. Maybe find another two or three, but not twenty-five," said Kepler.

"Fallon, you'd better find your people and have them ready to go."

"Sir," said Fallon, "there are regulations that cover the use of pilots, the amount of rest they are required to get, and the length of time they can fly each day and in a running, thirty-day period."

"Fine," said Gerber. "Anyone around paying any attention to those rules and regulations?"

Fallon shook his head.

"Then get with it." Gerber turned and left the room. As he walked down the hall, he told Kepler, "I want to be ready to get out to that hamlet tomorrow morning. I doubt we'll find anything of use, but we'd better go look."

"Yes, sir," said Kepler.

"What are we going to do?" asked Fetterman.

Gerber glanced at his watch and saw that it was nearly three in the morning. "Too late to head back downtown for some sleep there. Guess we can catch some here."

"And Miss Morrow?" asked Fetterman. "She seemed . . . distracted tonight."

"Robin and I have talked it all out now. She's probably asleep. Besides, we'll be back tomorrow afternoon. I can talk to her then."

"If you think that's best," said Fetterman.

"I think that's best, Master Sergeant."

ONCE THEY HAD FINISHED their work on Can Me To, the NVA headed for the jungle to the west of the hamlet. Nhu was in the rear, watching their trail, but none of the villagers seemed inclined to follow. That wasn't surprising. The villagers never followed. Government troops and the Americans, if they were around, sometimes tried to track them, but never the villagers. They were content to let the VC, the NVA, and everyone else walk in, force them to obey their orders and let them leave without voicing a protest.

They moved a couple of miles from the village and then halted. They fanned out along the path they had followed, taking positions to form an L-shaped ambush. Nhu was at the far end of it, anchoring that leg. If anyone showed up, his job was to make sure that no one escaped by running the way they had come, and to prevent a counterattack along the flank.

Once they had settled in, Nhu took a deep drink from his canteen, nearly emptying it. He knew it was a mistake to drink that much of his water, but he couldn't help himself. He was thirsty. Quick hikes through the jungle, terrorism in the villages, and waiting for the enemy always did that to him. Scared him and made him thirsty.

He crouched on one knee as he had been taught in North Vietnam. That kept him awake because it was impossible to sleep in that position. Listening carefully to the night sounds of the jungle around him, the scraping of small claws and the shrill cries of the creatures moving in the dark, also kept him alert. If he heard something unnatural, something human, he could slip to a prone position and be ready to fire at the enemy.

Now there was nothing to do but crouch in the humid depths of the jungle and wait. Let the sweat created by the march dry slowly, cooling him as the jungle shifted and shimmied, first under the harsh cruel light of the moon, and then the fiery reds and oranges of the coming sun. There was a chill in the air and there were wisps of white blowing on the light breeze from the west. The white, smokelike fog that wrapped the low, wet areas and the tops of the trees drifted silently, sometimes obscuring parts of the ground.

Nhu heard a quiet rustling to the right, among the rotting leaves and decaying plants. The scraping sound told him a snake was slithering away from him. Normally he would have been up and moving, but not tonight. He had to stay where he was, motionless, so that he didn't betray his position. Just stick where he was and hope the snake didn't sense his body heat and come hunting toward him.

Then there was silence. The almost constant booming of American artillery stopped suddenly. The roar of jets disappeared, and the popping of helicopter rotors vanished too. The quiet settled in on them then, wrapping them.

Nhu sat back, resting his backside on the heel of his right foot. He bowed his head like a man in prayer and listened to the jungle. Moisture dripped from the leaves above him. He heard a rattling in the bush, but nothing human. The war was over for a few minutes, at least in that small section of Vietnamese jungle. All was quiet.

Nhu felt himself relaxing, felt his eyes burning and knew that he was close to sleep. He forced himself upright and blinked rapidly. He wanted to rub his eyes and walk around to wake up, but couldn't. He had to force himself to stay awake with mental effort alone.

And then, when he thought he would fall asleep, the sky began to pale in the east. The stars faded, almost disappearing as the charcoal crept higher and the horizon turned gray.

Nhu shook his head slowly, blinked his eyes and then stifled a yawn. His body ached from the enforced inactivity. His muscles were stiff and his joints were sore.

But the good news was that no one seemed inclined to follow. The villagers had stayed in their hootches, afraid to come out. The Americans had not arrived and the South Vietnamese puppet soldiers would still be sleeping. They had completed their mission and had gotten away.

Van slipped along the line as the jungle began to brighten and the dark shadows began to take on real shape. The tops of trees, the branches of the bushes were suddenly defined. Van loomed from one of them and whispered, "We go in a little while. Back to our base."

Nhu nodded his understanding. He'd learned not to talk unless it was absolutely necessary.

FALLON LEFT THE SOG building, stepping out into the muggy night. Sweat blossomed on his forehead and dripped under his arms before he'd taken more than half a dozen steps. He reached the edge of the tarmac and stopped, staring into the lights of Tan Son Nhut.

The airfield's runways and taxiways were outlined in light. The hangars had lights on the fronts of them, and the various towers, both control and radio, had flashing beacons. To the east was a bright glow that marked Saigon.

He stood there, staring at a sandbagged revetment that protected an F-4 Phantom and the small yellow truck that was parked in front of it. Two men were working on the aircraft. Fallon had no idea what they were doing. Flying helicopters and flying jet fighters were two different things. Special skills had to be brought to each job, and while he could probably control the jet well enough to get it down, he knew that he wouldn't be able to fly it for very long.

A fix-winged pilot stuck into a helicopter would have a real chore. If he kept the helicopter flying fast enough, treating it like an airplane, he too, could probably land it. But there was no way that a man who had never flown a helicopter could hover it. That was a finesse move that required almost nonexistent movements to hold the helicopter steady over a single location while it tried to go in several different directions.

His instructor in flight school had told him to just think of making the moves, and the minute twitchings of the hands and feet were often enough to hold the helicopter steady. But to do it right, the pilot had to anticipate the movements of the helicopter, the wind and the air turbulence so that the corrections could be made almost before they were even necessary.

Hovering was not a simple thing to do. Slow and easy was the key. Fallon laughed out loud as he realized that standing there, thinking about the techniques of hovering was not getting the other pilots located.

He walked between the SOG building and a hangar to a dirt road. He followed it back to the east and Hotel Three. He located the officers' club, entered through the double door, walked past the lock boxes set against the wall for weapons, and stepped into the club proper. There were only a few people in it. Air Force pilots in flight suits eating breakfast. A single waitress who moved among them slowly. And no sign of his helicopter pilots.

Fallon left then, turned along the darkened street and walked toward the visiting officers' quarters. It made sense that the pilots would be there after their bout of drinking.

The VOQ was a single-story building. He entered through a double door and came to a front desk set to one side. A bored clerk sat behind the desk. It was a cramped room with a single chair near a window. A hallway led to the rooms, and there was another room off to the side that contained more chairs, a TV, and a table covered with beat-up copies of *Penthouse*, *Playboy* and *Time*.

Fallon moved to the front desk, leaned on it and stared at the clerk, who seemed to be asleep. Without opening his eyes, the man asked, "You want something?"

"Trying to find my pilots. Helicopter pilots."

"Yeah," said the clerk. "Try room one two seven. I think one of them is in there."

"You could look in your book," said Fallon.

The clerk opened his eyes and then rubbed a hand through his thick black hair. "Could, but that would tell me the same thing. Gave you a room number. They're all back there, grouped together."

"Thank you," said Fallon.

He walked down the hallway. The floor was dirty plywood, as were the walls, which were painted a light blue. From some of the rooms he could hear snoring, and from one came a feminine giggle. Obviously no one cared if the men had women in the rooms with them.

He came to a corner and turned to the left, entering another hallway that looked like the first. He found room one two seven and tapped on the door. Naturally there was no answer. He tried again, harder, and when no one appeared he banged on it, rattling it.

From another room someone shouted, "Knock it the fuck off, asshole."

Fallon felt the sweat bead on his forehead. He was suddenly uncomfortably hot and didn't have any idea of what to do. He didn't want to irritate anyone else.

He raised his hand to knock again and the door opened. Stockton, looking sleepy, blinked in the light from the hall and then asked, "What?"

"We've got a takeoff at eight. We need to alert the others and get them ready."

Stockton turned and disappeared into the room. Fallon waited for a moment and then pushed his way in. Stockton was sitting on the bed, trying to see the time.

"Little after five," said Fallon.

"Christ, we could catch another hour, hour and a half."

"Look," said Fallon, "you'll have to alert the others. Tell them to meet us at the SOG building and we'll ride over to Hotel Three for the choppers."

"Helicopters," said Stockton automatically. "We call them helicopters."

"Listen," snapped Fallon, his voice rising. "I'm a captain, and I'm trying to get you to get word to the others."

The voice from the hall screamed, "I'm a major and I'm trying to get some fucking sleep here."

Fallon looked toward the hall and lowered his voice. "I take it that everyone has checked in here."

Stockton shook his head, figured that Fallon couldn't see it in the dark. "Only the pilots are here. I don't know where the ACs are."

"What the hell do you mean you don't know where the ACs are?"

"Just what I said. They didn't come here to check in. I went over to the club, but they weren't there, either."

"God damn it!" shouted Fallon.

"One more word," came the voice, "and I'm coming out there, you asshole."

Fallon dropped his voice. "Then where are they?"

"Christ," said Stockton. "That's not my problem. My problem is to ride around with Newhawser and try not to get killed. You're the RLO."

"RLO?" said Fallon.

"Real live officer. I'm a warrant and I fly airplanes. I don't have to play the other games. Now, if you'll get the fuck out of here, I'll get some sleep."

"But where are the others?"

"That's your problem," said Stockton, yawning again. He scratched his belly.

Fallon was silent for a moment, watching. Then he said, "I want you to get the others up and over to the SOG building."

"Now?"

"Of course, now," said Fallon. "Do you think that the ACs might have gone downtown?"

"I don't know what they might have done. All I know is that they're not here."

"Shit," said Fallon. "What am I going to do?"

"That's your problem," said Stockton. He reached over and turned on the light.

"Shit," said Fallon again.

"Shut the fuck up," said the major in another room. "I'm trying to sleep."

6

THE SOG BUILDING

Gerber sat in the briefing room, studying the map that Kepler had left for him. Trying to second-guess the VC or NVA was going to be difficult because he didn't know what their mission was or where their camp might be hidden. The Cambodian border was too far to the west to be of real value to them. The American camp at Dau Tieng separated Can Me To from Nui Ba Den, and if they moved too far to the south, they would be into the swamps south of Highway One where there was no real cover to protect them from the Americans.

But even knowing all that, it didn't help much. The rubber plantations had been a VC stronghold and now belonged to the North Vietnamese. The Boi Loi Woods and the Hobo Woods provided protection, and there were rumors of tunnel systems near Cu Chi that had yet to be explored. Plenty of places for the enemy to hide. It would take a month with a brigade and four hundred aircraft to search properly, and even then there was no guarantee they would find the enemy.

Fetterman appeared in the doorway carrying two cups of coffee. "Care for something to drink, Captain?"

Gerber waved him in and pointed at the map. "They'll be long gone by the time we hit the field tomorrow, or rather, this morning."

"Uh-huh," said Fetterman, handing over one of the cups. He sat down and leaned back. "Kepler said that his agent told him the VC moved off toward the west. Check that. The NVA moved off to the west."

Gerber picked up the cup and took a sip. "He sure they were NVA?"

"Dressed as VC," said Fetterman. "The man said they had too much discipline, were all armed with AKs and all had that damned NVA haircut."

"So where'd they go after they hit the village?"

Fetterman took a drink of his coffee, then set the cup on the table. He leaned back and closed his eyes. "Naturally any report we get from the locals wouldn't be worth much. SOP to leave in one direction and then change direction as soon as you're out of sight."

"Which doesn't answer the question."

"What we need," said Fetterman, "is a complete report on every such incident in the last month. Plot them on the map, then see if it tells us anything about the location of their base."

"We won't be able to get that until tomorrow, and it won't help us now."

"So we land, follow the trail into the jungle and see what we can see."

Gerber picked up his cup and then stood up, walking around the table. He was quiet for several minutes, stopping his pacing long enough to look at the maps and then starting again. Finally he said, "Logically they would operate out of Cambodia. Hit there and then run back to keep us away from them."

"Except the distance to Cambodia from Can Me To is prohibitive."

"Which means they've got a base inside of South Vietnam. That's as far as it goes."

Fetterman finished his coffee. "That may be enough. Especially since we have those choppers."

"So the only thing we could do is fly out there tomorrow and see what we can learn. Providing Kepler can turn up the troops we need. If not, we wait for the strikers from Muc Hoa."

There was a tapping at the door and Fallon stuck his head in. "Captain Gerber, we might have another problem. I don't know what happened to the aircraft commanders. They seem to have disappeared."

"Disappeared?" said Fetterman. "How long they been in Vietnam?"

"That important?"

"How long?" echoed Gerber.

"Six months, eight months. A long time," said Fallon.

"They go downtown to Tu Do Street?" asked Gerber.

Fallon shook his head. "I don't think so. I would think they'd stay on base."

"Sure," said Gerber. He leaned around so that he was looking out the door. "Hey, Kepler! Get in here."

Kepler came down the hall and asked, "You bellered at me, Captain?"

"This man seems to have lost half his pilots. You wouldn't know where they are, would you?"

"They go to the club on base or they go off base?" asked Kepler.

Fallon shrugged. "As far as I know, they stayed on base."

"As far as you know," repeated Kepler.

Gerber cut in. "He doesn't keep very good track of his troops."

"Yes, sir. You've checked the club already?" said Kepler.

"No one in there but some Air Force pilots eating their breakfast. Checked the VOQ too. None of them are there. The peter pilots are, but none of the ACs."

"Well, I doubt they'd all get lucky at once. That leaves only a couple of places. Let me make a couple of calls and I'll see what I can learn."

"Thank you, Sergeant," said Fallon.

Gerber checked the time. "Make it snappy. I want to be in the field by nine this morning. Providing you've gotten the troops we need and we can find the missing pilots," said Gerber.

"Yes, sir. I've got twenty men arriving here at zero seven three zero, with equipment, weapons and ammo, ready to go crush Communism."

"Now all we need are the pilots," said Fetterman.

Kepler disappeared again. Fallon sat down and said, "We really didn't plan for anything until tomorrow."

"There any more coffee?" asked Gerber.

"I'll get it," said Fetterman. He walked out, and returned a few moments later, handing one of the cups to Gerber.

Kepler stuck his head around the door. "I've found the pilots, but I'm going to need one of you to help get them. One of you officers."

"Oh, shit," said Fallon.

NEWHAWSER SAT ON HIS COT in the cell and wondered how long they were going to be kept there. He leaned his elbows on his knees and stared at the concrete floor. It was filthy. Crushed cigarette butts, spit and dried vomit. Newhawser shook his head and said, "It's not fair."

Rice, who was fingering a bruise on the side of his face again said, "Figures they'd arrest us. Air Force starts the fight and Air Force mediates it. We're in jail."

Newhawser stood up and grabbed the bars. He looked into the corridor at the steel door, at the small window with bars set in it. A shadow passed in front of it.

"Hey!" shouted Newhawser. "Hey!"

A face appeared and asked, "What do you want?"

"How about letting us out of here?"

"No way," said the man.

"Then get someone out here. Someone in authority."

Without a word, the face vanished. Newhawser stared at the window and then turned toward Rice. "Looks like they're going to ignore us."

But then the door opened and a man in jungle fatigues and wearing major leaves entered. He walked right to the cell and stared down at Newhawser.

"I'm in authority here. What do you want?"

Newhawser rubbed his chin. "Sir, we didn't start the fight."

"I understand that one of your men was standing on a stool demanding a woman."

"Yes, sir. That's true. But it was an Air Force pilot who started the fight, which was over by the time the Air Police got there."

"Your man insulted a number of the women."

"Not really," said Newhawser. "But then, is that any reason to throw us in jail?"

The major looked at the sergeant who had followed him and said, "That true?"

"Well, sir," said the man, "there wasn't a fight going on when we got there. And they came along peacefully."

"Shit," said the major. "There's no reason to keep these guys here. Release them."

"Yes, sir."

The major turned and faced Newhawser. "You spread the word that if I hear any of you in here again, I'll throw the book at you. You look at someone cross-eyed, and it's all over for you."

Rice started to say, "But that's not—"

Newhawser cut him off. "Yes, sir. We'll probably be too busy anyway. Or we'll go downtown."

"That's fine." He snapped his fingers and pointed at the door. "Let them out, Sergeant."

"Yes, sir."

The sergeant opened the door, moved to the right and unlocked the second. The major waited until they were all released. The pilots followed him out into a booking area. There was a waist-high counter, a camera, fingerprinting station, and step-up where the pictures were taken.

The major turned to them and repeated, "I see any of you in here again, I'll throw the book at you."

"Yes, sir," said Newhawser.

The sergeant pulled out several large manila envelopes and pushed them across the counters. The pilots sorted through them, got their belongings and started toward the door.

"You got to sign for that," grumbled the sergeant.

As they did, the major said, "I'm feeling merciful tonight. Don't count on it again."

"Yes, sir," said Newhawser.

Outside, in the muggy heat of dawn, Rice asked, "What do we do now?"

"Over to the VOQ and catch some sleep," said Newhawser. "What else?"

"Sounds good," said Rice. He looked at the other three pilots. "Any objections?"

Cruz said, "How about something to eat first?"

"Food first and then sleep," said Hoskinson.

"All right then, let's go eat," said Newhawser.

FETTERMAN DROVE THEM over to the Air Police building. Gerber and Fallon went in while Fetterman waited outside. They found the major, who told them that the helicopter pilots had been released.

"So where did they go?" asked Gerber.

"Looking for something to eat," said the major.

Fallon stood there for a moment. "You have a lima lima to Cu Chi?"

"Sergeant," said the major, "take the captain to the switchboard and help him make his call."

"Yes, sir."

As they left, Gerber said, "What in the hell is going on here?"

The major pointed toward a door. "Let's go into my office. You want some coffee?"

"No, thank you."

The office was tiny. There was a small gray desk, a single chair for the visitors and a short bookcase filled with black loose-leaf binders. There was a single picture on the wall. Phantoms attacking a jungle outpost.

"Sit," said the major.

As he did, Gerber noticed a nameplate that said, "Major Jason Baker, USAF."

"Just one question, Major. Why'd you arrest the Army pilots?"

Baker sat down in his chair, which squeaked badly. He tented his fingers under his chin. "Mainly because they were the odd man out. Everyone else was Air Force. The situation was defused by taking the Army men out of the club. That's the one reason that I let them walk out of here earlier. It was the only fair thing to do."

"Wish you'd hung on to them for another thirty minutes. That would have made my life a little easier."

"Just what is going on here?" asked Baker.

Gerber shrugged. "What can I tell you? We've some things to do and we need the pilots to help."

"My advice to you, Captain," said Baker, "is to keep them out of the club."

Gerber shook his head. "That's just stupid."

Baker looked at the Special Forces officer and then laughed. "Well, it was a thought."

"Not much of one," said Gerber.

Fallon appeared then. "I've finished. Let's go find the pilots."

Gerber stood up and said, "Thank you, Major."

Baker held out a hand. "I'd check the club for them. That's probably where they are."

They left and found Fetterman sitting in his jeep, his hands on the wheel, waiting. "You find them?"

"Possibly," said Gerber. "Take us to the officers' club."

They drove over there. The base was beginning to come awake. There were more people out. Men walking along the roads. Lights were burning in a number of the buildings. More jeeps and trucks were around.

They pulled up outside the officers' club. Fallon jumped out of the back. "I'll check inside and see if my people are in there."

"Go ahead," said Gerber.

Fallon entered the doors, stopped and looked around. There were a number of people in there, eating. At first he didn't see his men, and then spotted them at a table in the rear, out of easy line of sight. He walked over to them.

"Glad that I could find you."

Rice looked up and grinned. "How's it going, Captain? Care to join us?"

"I want you all to get over to the SOG building immediately. We've a takeoff time of zero eight hundred."

Newhawser looked at his watch, saw that takeoff was more than two hours away and said, "Plenty of time for breakfast. The peter pilots are supposed to preflight anyway."

"I want you at the SOG building, now."

Rice said, "You're creating a scene. Sit down and be quiet."

Fallon pulled out a chair and dropped into it. He glanced into the faces of each of the aircraft commanders, wondering what in the hell they were thinking about. Fighting in the officers' club, drinking before they got their assignments for the next day, and then disappearing completely. Getting arrested for starting the fight.

"I've talked to Major Devane and he's not pleased with the way things have started. He's talking about Article Fifteens for each of you . . ."

"Nope," said Rice.

"What'd you mean, nope? You can't refuse an Article Fifteen," said Fallon. "As soon as we're back to Cu Chi, he's going to talk to each of you about it."

Hoskinson leaned forward, elbows on the table. "Of course you can refuse an Article Fifteen," he said quietly. "Everyone can refuse an Article Fifteen. You have the right to demand a court-martial."

"That'd be stupid," said Fallon.

"Nope," said Spilman. "It's brilliant. Oh, by the way, you'll have to rescind our AC orders while we all wait for the court-martial."

Newhawser picked up the ball and ran with it. "Just think, no more flying until DEROS. Gentlemen, it seems that I have survived my year in Vietnam."

"I think this calls for a drink," said Rice.

"You can't drink until after five," said Fallon, losing control suddenly.

"Hell, it's after five, now."

"I mean in the afternoon," said Fallon.

"Fuck it," said Rice. "I say that since we're no longer ACs we all get drunk."

"You're still ACs," said Fallon.

"No, sir," said Rice. "There's no regulation that demands we become aircraft commanders. And if I'm going to be court-martialed, I sure as hell don't deserve to be an aircraft commander."

Fallon lost his temper. "We have a takeoff at eight. I would suggest that you be there in time for it. In fact, you'd better be at the SOG building inside of an hour for a briefing. Do you understand that?''

Newhawser looked at the others. "Do we understand that?" He turned his attention to Fallon. "I think we understand that. Completely. Now, why don't you let us eat our breakfast in peace."

Fallon stood up. "You people have your orders." He turned and moved toward the door.

As he approached it, he heard one of them say, "Well that was nice of the old boy. Glad he could stop by to say good morning to us."

Outside he climbed into the rear of the jeep. Gerber turned and faced him. "You find them?"

"They're eating breakfast. They'll be over to the SOG building in about an hour for a briefing."

Fetterman started the jeep's engine. "What are you going to do for a briefing?"

"What do you mean?" asked Fallon.

"He means," said Gerber, "that all you need to know is where to land and when to pick us up. Not much of a briefing. We hadn't planned anything formal."

"Oh. That'll do just fine."

Fetterman dropped the jeep into gear and said, "I hope Derek's found us some troopies. Otherwise we're basically fucked."

"Basically," agreed Gerber.

7

HOTEL THREE

Kepler had found the twenty men, Fallon had gotten all the pilots over to the helicopters, and all the crew chiefs and gunners had been waiting there when they arrived. Gerber and Fetterman, dressed in jungle fatigues and carrying M-16s borrowed from the stocks at the SOG building, were walking across the grass toward the helicopters.

As they neared, a man ran from the terminal and announced, "You can't leave your aircraft here again."

Gerber looked at him. "They're not my aircraft and they won't be here tonight. Don't worry about it."

"Yes, sir."

Kepler came forward and spoke to Gerber. "I've briefed the troops on this. Standard sweep through the village."

"Short sweep, just to see if there's anything to learn there. If not, we'll get out and head back here."

"Yes, sir."

"Divide them up into equal loads. You ride in the trail aircraft. Tony, you're in number three."

"Got it."

Gerber approached the lead chopper where Fallon stood leaning against the cockpit door. The cargo doors were open and shoved back. The M-60 machine guns were mounted. One crewman lay on the troop seat sleeping. Another was sprawled on the floor, using a chicken plate for a pillow.

"You about ready to go?" asked Gerber.

"All set. We'd like to stop off at Cu Chi first to refuel," said Fallon.

"I'd like to hit the field first, if that's possible," said Gerber.

The man who'd been sleeping on the troop seat sat up and said, "Let me see that map again." He studied it and then said, "That shouldn't be a problem. We've got enough fuel to get us into Tay Ninh or Dau Tieng if we want. I take it there'll be no arty prep."

"It's a friendly village," said Gerber.

"Sure," said the man. "Friendly."

Fallon stepped in. "Captain Gerber, this is Mr. Rice, one of the aircraft commanders."

Now Gerber grinned. "Had some trouble last night, huh?"

"A little."

"Let the Air Force win," he said shaking his head in mock disapproval. "Let them just cart you off."

"Didn't want to cause a whole lot of additional trouble. Besides, that got us out of there without paying for the last round of drinks. Nobody's thought of that yet."

Gerber let that slide. He got back on track. "Then there's no trouble getting in and out of the village?"

"Hell, sir, it's a piece of cake. Plenty of open ground. Only thing we might want to do is coordinate the landing with our guns for a little cover, just in case."

"Even in a friendly village?"

"If it's so friendly, what's the purpose of going out there?" asked Rice.

"Good point." Gerber looked at Fallon. "You'll have to arrange that."

"No problem."

"Are we ready now?" asked Gerber.

"Whenever you're ready, Captain," said Fallon. "Load them up."

Gerber waved a hand, motioning the soldiers into the helicopters. As they climbed on board, the crew chiefs untied the rotor blades, swinging them out. Gerber watched the activity for a few moments, then jumped into the rear of the Huey.

Rice was keenly aware of his throbbing head as he walked around to the nose of the aircraft. He opened the access hatch and tossed his baseball cap into it, then moved back around and climbed up into the left-hand seat. The right seat had been set up for the aircraft commander, but most of them rode on the left side because they could see better out the windshield.

As he strapped himself in, he wondered if that was the real reason. Airplanes were set up for the captain or the aircraft commander to ride on the left. Maybe some of the helicopter pilots thought helicopters should be the same.

Dismissing the thought, Rice flipped the switches, working through the start-up procedure quickly. The main function was to make sure that everything was shut off until it was time to start the engine. Then the battery switch, the start generator, the start fuel and a couple of other things were turned on again. It was done to make sure that the radio and navigation gear weren't ruined by a sudden surge of power.

He leaned to the right, rolled on the throttle to the flight idle detent, set it so that he could roll it off if necessary, and then yelled, "Clear!"

The crew chief and the door gunner both looked right and left and then to the rear. Both shouted, "Clear."

Rice pulled the trigger that was set under the collective. The turbine began to whine. He checked the instruments and then focused on the gas producer gauge, making sure that the needle didn't spike into the red for a hot start. He also watched the engine RPM.

Finally, with everything in the green, he rolled on the throttle and used the button on the collective to take the engine RPM to six thousand. With the engine roaring, Rice turned and plucked his flight helmet off the hook just behind his head. He didn't bother buckling the chin strap.

That done, he flipped on the radios and everything else. He glanced at Fallon and said, "You want to get us clearance to take off? Flight of five."

Fallon nodded.

Rice then turned and looked into the cargo compartment. There were six American soldiers there. Each had an M-16 pointed toward the top of the helicopter. The theory was that an accidental discharge would do the least damage if the round went through the roof.

"We're cleared to go. Take off to the south."

Rice keyed the mike. "Lead's coming up to a hover." He sucked in some pitch and pointed the helicopter toward the south. "Lead's on the go."

He dumped the nose and took off over the south end of Hotel Three. They continued to climb to five hundred feet. Out the left side of the helicopter was the urban sprawl of Saigon. There was a golden haze over the city that looked like the smog that sometimes hid Los Angeles.

"Beginning a descent," said Rice.

"You're joined with five."

"Roger, five."

They descended, low-leveled until they crossed Highway One. Then they turned to the west, flew through the huge opening in the tree line that marked the border of the zone used as the approach paths to Tan Son Nhut. Beyond that they climbed out and crossed Highway One again so that they would be on the northern side. The rules of the road applied to the helicopters in the air.

As they reached fifteen hundred feet, Rice leveled off and reached over to turn on the ADF. With the rock and roll filling his earphones, he asked, "You want to take it?"

Fallon put the map into the case at the end of the console and then reached out for the cyclic and collective. "I've got it," he said.

Rice let go and sat back. He flipped his radio over. "Lead's going to eighty knots."

He pulled the map out of the case and opened it. He studied the terrain under him and then said, "You're going to have to bear to right a little more. When we get close, you'll see the Mushroom, that is a series of bends in the river that look like a mushroom, the cap pointing to the south."

"I know where it is."

"Good," said Rice. He folded the map and stuffed it into the map case. He leaned back, his head propped up by the armor seat and closed his eyes. There was a pounding in the back of his head, and his eyes felt hot, grainy. Closing them eased the discomfort. He opened them a moment later.

While Fallen flew on, trying to maintain eighty knots and fifteen hundred feet, Rice switched over to the company FM. He contacted operations and asked that a gun team be sent for the insertion.

"Wait one," came the reply.

Rice lifted his hand and grabbed the handle above his head. He watched the scene below him. A blue, hazy scene with smoke from a fire off near the Song Sai Gon. He could pick out the Hobo Woods, the huge French-owned rubber plantation near Dau Tieng and, of course, Nui Ba Den.

"This is Operations."

"Go," said Rice, stepping on the floor button.

"That's a negative on the guns. We have two teams tied up on other missions."

"Roger," said Rice. He lifted his foot off the button. "Jesus Christ in a bobsled."

"We're getting close," said Fallon.

Rice nodded and glanced toward Nui Ba Den on the left and the Mushroom to the right. The trees, the bushes, the brush, weren't as thick here as up in the central Highlands. It was forest rather than thick jungle. Scraggly trees and sickly bushes. Open areas of rice paddy or bare ground. There was an almost perfect circle, the ground inside it beaten down. The remains of an abandoned fire-support base. The outlines of the perimeter, the bunkers and the various structures were still visible.

Rice didn't like landing in that area without gun support. He spoke to Fallon on the intercom. "Village is off to the left now. You see it?"

"I see two or three," said Fallon.

"That's the Can Me complex. The one you're interested in is to the south. See it?"

"Right."

Rice sat up. "You're not getting gun support so we have to run this ourselves."

"I understand."

"Surface winds are probably close to what they were in Saigon. We'll want to land, north to south on the eastern side of the village." Rice pointed at the windshield. "That puts the closest trees more than two, three hundred yards from us. Only point we'll have to worry about will be the village itself."

"Suppression, sir?" said the crew chief.

Rice looked back over the seat. "Normal rules."

"Yes, sir."

"Whenever you're ready," said Rice.

Fallon shrugged and then squeezed the mike button. "Let's do it now."

"Then I've got it," said Rice.

"Let me take it in," said Fallon.

"Nope, I've got it."

"You've got it."

Rice took control. He keyed the radio. "Flight, come up a heavy right. We have normal rules."

A moment later there was a call from Trail. "You have a heavy right."

"Turning inbound."

Rice came back on the cyclic slightly, letting some of the airspeed bleed off. He picked out a landing point and aimed for it. His eyes kept moving, checking the instruments and the ground outside. He saw movement in the village, but nothing that looked threatening. There was smoke on the western side and more activity there, but no young men running for the trees with rifles in their hands.

A bird took off in a flash of white feathers, coming up suddenly in front of the chopper. Instinctively, Fallon threw up a hand as if to protect his face. Rice held the cyclic steady, ignoring the distraction. If the bird came through the windshield there was nothing he could do, but a sudden control movement with four helicopters behind him could be disastrous. He could cause a midair collision. Once the approach was started, they were locked into it.

The bird hit the side of the chopper and seemed to explode. Feathers, blood and bone splashed the windshield, making it hard to see. But Rice didn't alter the approach. He continued to stare at his touchdown point, aware of the bird, aware of the running people and the smoke, of the trees around the village and the landing point.

At a hundred feet he pulled slowly, steadily back on the cyclic, flaring. The nose came up and Rice lost sight of the touchdown point. The airspeed dropped off and they began to settle toward the ground faster. As that happened, Rice leveled the skids and found himself almost hovering three feet above his landing point. With a single fluid motion, he dropped the collective, used the pedals and the cyclic and touched the ground.

An instant later came, "You're down with five and you're unloaded."

"Roger. Lead's on the go." Rice pulled up the collective and shoved the cyclic forward. They came off the ground and were racing along suddenly.

"You're off with five. No fire."

"Roger, that. Climbing out."

"Piece of cake," said the trail pilot on the radio.

"For us," said Rice, using the intercom. Then, "You've got it."

Fallon put his hands on the controls. "I've got it."

As THEY APPROACHED the village, the crew chief leaned around from his well and shouted, "We're inbound now."

Gerber nodded and slapped the shoulder of the man next to him, but the soldier was aware of the situation. He had touched the selector switch on his weapon, felt at the strap of his helmet and then looked nervously at Gerber. He grinned, showing yellowed, broken teeth.

The ground seemed to rush up at them. Gerber wished the chopper wasn't making so much noise. He wished he could communicate with the others, but the roar of the turbine and the popping of the blades made it difficult to talk. The men closest could hear him if they leaned toward him and Gerber shouted loud enough. Those more than two feet away would never hear.

Gerber raised a thumb and then turned toward the open cargo compartment door. This was the worst time. Enemy firing could bring down the chopper before Gerber and the men with him knew what happened. They were the most vulnerable now because they didn't know what was out there. An ambush could kill them all in an instant.

Then suddenly they were on the ground with the crew chief yelling at them over the roar of the engine, "Get out! Get out! Get out!"

As the skids touched the ground, lost in the two-foot-high elephant grass, Gerber leaped out. He ran five or six yards from the helicopter and crouched, facing toward the trees more than two hundred yards off.

Behind him the helicopters lifted. Dust, debris, loose grass and dried leaves were caught in the whirlwind of the rotor wash. The wind hit his back with enough force to stagger him. He closed his eyes against the swirling, blowing dust. In an instant the wind was gone and the noise was fading to the south.

He glanced to the right and saw the helicopters disappearing in the distance. Gerber was on his feet then, moving to the west. Fetterman had his men moving, as did Kepler. They were spreading out now, on line, moving straight for the village.

Gerber saw it all spread out in front of him. There was a hint of smoke in the air. He was suddenly hot, sweating. He was tense, wondering why the people were suddenly missing from the scene. He reached up with his thumb and flipped the sector switch from safe to single-shot.

Fetterman and three of the men with him moved forward quickly. They stopped at the edge of the village, crouching down, their weapons pointing at the village.

The flanks slipped out, curling around toward the edges of the village. Gerber and the men with him filled in behind Fetterman, and when they were in position, Fetterman was up and moving again.

It wasn't much of a village. Mud-and-thatch hootches, mud fences and dirty pathways between the small structures. An ox cart, missing a wheel, sat off to the right side. There was an ox pen near one of the hootches, and the stench from the manure blew back in their faces. A couple of cooking fires were burning, pots hung over them, but there were no people tending them.

As Fetterman filtered into the village, Gerber followed
They swept through from east to west, coming to the body of
the dead school-teacher. Fetterman crouched over it and
reached down, touching her throat. He shook his head, confirming that she was dead.

He stood and looked toward the remains of the school
building. Smoke was billowing from the rubble. Debris from
the walls was scattered over the ground. There were bits of
wood, papers, books and the remnants of the South Vietnamese flag.

They reached the end of the village and stopped. The men
automatically took up defensive positions. Fetterman approached Gerber and then waited for Kepler.

"I don't like this," said Fetterman. "Everyone's scared."

"That's to be expected," said Gerber.

"No, sir," said Fetterman. "It's worst than I thought. They
want nothing to do with us. Normally someone would come
out to see what we're doing, but they won't even do that."

"I could ask my man," said Kepler, "but that would burn
him."

Gerber looked at the master sergeant. "If they refuse to
come out, it might mean the VC are still around."

Fetterman looked into the jungle and then at the ground
around them. "We could search for the trail."

Gerber crouched, suddenly feeling as if someone was
watching him. The skin on the back of his neck was crawling
and he could almost feel the bullet striking him.

"Do it," he said.

Fetterman took two of the men and walked to the edge of
the jungle and began searching the ground carefully. After a
few moments Fetterman returned.

"Got it."

"Take the point," said Gerber.

"Yes, sir."

As Fetterman slipped into the jungle, the rest of the men formed a line and followed. They moved slowly, carefully, the men searching the trees around them. Two men fell toward the rear with Kepler. They watched their trail, making sure that no one was following them.

Once they were all into the trees, Fetterman stopped moving. He crouched at the head of the column and waited for Gerber to catch him.

"Twelve guys passed through here about seven hours ago."

Gerber knelt and looked at the footprint that Fetterman had located. Tire tread from the Ho Chi Minh sandals that the enemy soldiers wore.

"We could be walking into an ambush," said Fetterman.

"I know that," said Gerber. "You and two, three guys could stay on the trail while the rest of us paralleled your course about fifty yards to the right."

"Yes, sir, you could. But I don't like being set up without having more information about the enemy."

"I don't like it either," said Gerber. "But we are supposed to find these guys."

"We could retreat to the village and check the situation out there."

Gerber stared up the trail, studying the terrain. Stunted trees, bushes with dry leaves that rattled in the light breeze. A few thin vines hanging from the branches of the trees. Rough, broken ground. Plenty of places for an ambush to hide, but then, plenty of opportunities to take cover.

With the sun now high overhead, the jungle floor was well lighted, making it easier to spot the things that didn't fit in naturally. The sun was also baking the ground, making it difficult to continue. The heat and humidity sapped everyone's strength.

Gerber realized what he was doing. He didn't want to continue and was searching for excuses not to. This was a haphazard mission thrown together because the enemy had attacked the village the night before. He was now working with a group of pilots he didn't know and grunts who were not trained by the Special Forces. He had no confidence in them because he had never seen them before they arrived at the helicopters, and he didn't know what training they'd had.

"Captain?" said Fetterman.

Gerber nodded and then said, "Let's do this. Up the trail another klick or two. See if we can learn anything. Or move until the trail peters out. Then return to the village for pickup."

"Yes, sir."

Fetterman and the two men with him started off again, following the path used by the NVA. They moved slowly, heads swiveling right and left, searching for enemy soldiers. Fetterman stepped carefully, easing his foot down, waiting for the sudden snag of a trip wire or the pinpoint pressure of a booby trap on his foot.

They hadn't moved far when Fetterman stopped again. He searched the trees above them, looking for birds, listening to the sounds of the insects. A natural undercurrent to the noise of the forest. There was no indication that anyone was in the jungle with them, because the undercurrent hadn't been disturbed as it would be if there were others.

He waved one man forward and watched as he dodged right and left, taking a position near a fallen tree. He dropped to one knee, his weapon pointed down the trail in front of him. He continued to look around, searching for the enemy.

The second man leapfrogged forward, past the other soldier, and then jumped over a log without looking and without thinking. There was a click, a pause, and then an explosion. Black smoke and dust boiled upward.

"Oh, shit," said Fetterman, but he didn't run forward. He hesitated, waiting for a burst of machine-gun fire. That didn't happen. Instead came the groaning of the wounded man, and Fetterman knew that if the enemy had been close, they would be gone within minutes.

8

THE CARASEL HOTEL
SAIGON

Gerber hadn't returned. Of course. She'd known when Fetterman came and got him that he wouldn't be coming back. She'd hoped that he would, that the problem, whatever it was, would be a small one. It obviously hadn't been, because Gerber didn't reappear.

She had planned for his return, forcing herself off the bed and into the bathroom. Her original idea had been to get drunk and stay that way, but with Gerber gone, there was no point. And after what he had said to her, she wasn't convinced that the plan was a good one.

Instead she stumbled into the bathroom and turned on the faucets in the old Victorian-style tub. It was a monstrous thing with clawed feet and a rust stain on the front and near the drain. She turned on the hot water and then sat on the side, her fingers in the stream, waiting for it to heat up. When she could stand it no more, she adjusted the cold and then put the plug in the drain, letting the tub fill.

She pulled off her clothes, letting them fall to the floor of the bathroom. When the tub was filled, she shut off the water and then reached down to feel the temperature. Nice and hot. She climbed in, standing with the water over her ankles. Slowly she lowered herself. Once she was in, she leaned back and slipped down. The water covered her to the chin.

"Now," she said, not knowing exactly what she meant.

The thoughts that had provoked her all day were suddenly gone. The water was relaxing and there was a glow in her belly from the bourbon, and from the words spoken by Gerber. Her eyes were heavy but she resisted falling asleep. At least for a few moments.

It felt good, lying in the water and not worrying about her sister who was going to marry the doctor, or about her parents who seemed to think she had failed because she was a journalist. She just couldn't work up a good anger about it anymore. Someday they'd understand that her job wasn't as bad as they thought. She was a professional whose work was respected by her peers.

She sat up for a moment, let the water roll off her. It might have been a little too warm. Her skin was turning pink and her heart was pounding. Sweat beaded at her hairline and dripped down the side of her face. She reached up and plucked a washcloth from the rack and mopped her face with it.

Leaning back, the washcloth spread on her chest as if she were hiding herself from unseen eyes, she relaxed there, letting the water cool slowly. When the skin on her fingers began to wrinkle, she decided it was time to get out.

She dried herself, then looked with distaste at her clothes. They weren't dirty—they'd only been worn a couple of hours—but she just didn't want to get back in them. Instead she wrapped a towel around her waist and stepped to the mirror. Wiping the fog from it, she leaned close and looked at herself, finally turning and walking back to the bedroom.

At first she sat there, staring at the little black-and-white television that Gerber had bought, wondering whether to turn it on. Deciding that there couldn't be anything on that was worthwhile, she stood and walked to the air conditioner, turned it down and then returned to the bed, leaving the towel on the floor.

But when Gerber didn't return, she fell asleep, dozing fitfully until she realized that Gerber was not coming back that morning. Then she got up, used Gerber's toothbrush and put on her clothes again.

After leaving the hotel and returning to work, she moved through the city room and took her place at her desk. Instead of working, she sat there and stared at the blotter. After a few minutes a shadow fell across her desk.

She looked up. "What do you want, Mark?"

Hodges studied her face. "You get anything on that village elder who was murdered?"

Morrow shook her head. "I was going over to MACV, but I got sidetracked."

"Anything interesting?" asked Hodges.

"No. Talked to Gerber..."

"He know anything about it?"

"No."

Hodges parked a hip on the corner of her desk and stared down at her. "Did you even ask him?"

"No."

"Robin," said Hodges, sighing, "this is a news-gathering organization. We've got to gather the news or we don't have anything."

"Mark, I'm really not in the mood for a lecture on the reasons for our existence."

"Well," said Hodges, "the real reason I came over here is to let you know that a school-teacher was killed last night and her school was destroyed. The VC walked into the village, blew up the school and then killed her."

"Last night?" asked Morrow.

"About midnight or so."

"How do you know?"

Now Hodges smiled. "I have my sources, and obviously he is over in MACV."

"Are we going to do anything about it?"

"Meaning, us here?" asked Hodges.

"No damn it, the Army."

"I don't know. All I know is that acts of terrorism have been escalating. Since Tet, the VC haven't been operating on the scale they had been. Now it seems they're targeting specific people as an example. That might be the direction we want to follow."

Morrow reached over and pulled a notepad closer. She scribbled a few words. "Who's the contact over at MACV?"

"I can't burn my source."

"Oh, Christ, Mark, if you won't tell me, then I can't do anything."

"Look, there's going to be some kind of briefing this morning that will address this problem. Head over there, see what you can learn. Then, if you need a name, I'll give it to you."

Morrow nodded. For a moment she sat quietly, then asked, "You said this happened around midnight?"

"Something like that. We got word of it about midnight, so it must have been a little earlier. Why?"

Morrow shrugged. "I don't know. I might have something after all."

"You suggesting your Green Beret friend might have something to do with this?"

"I doubt that." She looked at her watch. "What time is the briefing?"

"Eleven. The Army doesn't want the reporters to have to get up too early."

"I'll head over there and see what I can come up with."

"Keep me posted," said Hodges.

Morrow stood up then. "I will."

FETTERMAN REACHED THE wounded man in a matter of seconds. He lay on his back, and his rifle was four feet away. One leg was doubled under him, the other splintered, the cloth of his jungle fatigues shredded and covered in blood. White bone showed through. A pool of blood was forming under him.

Fetterman hesitated, studying the jungle around him. The last thing he wanted was to leap into action and get cut down. VC booby traps were designed to wound and maim but not necessarily to kill. It stopped a unit when a man was wounded. It slowed pursuit. And a wounded man made good bait to draw out other, healthier soldiers. If a sniper was around, he could kill or wound several others if they tried to help the wounded man without checking the surrounding territory.

The moaning of the wounded man got louder. Fetterman pointed at the other soldier and then at the side of the fallen tree. The soldier moved forward, taking that position.

The rest of the men slipped forward, waiting for signals from Fetterman. He stopped them and then motioned for them to spread out for security. He got two men forward, including Gerber, to act as personal security and then leaped over the fallen tree. Rather than move forward, he crouched there, searching for the unseen enemy. Satisfied that no one was around, he looked at the wounded man again.

The booby trap had shredded the foot and the lower leg. The boot had been torn apart, bits of it hanging on the bloody mess. The bones of the foot and the shin were visible and he was bleeding badly. Fetterman straightened the other leg and saw that the shrapnel had damaged it. There were minor wounds to the thighs, and he suspected the backside and back also.

Fetterman stripped the lace from the man's good boot and looped it around the leg, using the handle of his knife to tighten it. As he did, he glanced at the time. He was aware of someone standing beside him. It was Gerber.

"How bad?" the captain asked.

"Real. We've got to get him out of here or he's had it. Loss of blood and shock."

"Can you move him?"

"I'd rather not."

Gerber pointed and then dropped his hand quickly. "We've a one ship LZ about fifty yards back."

"Get the ship in there, now," said Fetterman.

Gerber retreated, found the RTO crouched next to a tree and said, "Come up on six five decimal five."

The man complied and gave the handset to Gerber. Gerber squeezed it. "Hornet three three, Hornet three three, this is Zulu six."

"Go, six."

"Say location."

"Refueling point at Cu Chi."

"Roger. Break off one aircraft for emergency Medevac west of our LZ."

"Roger, that. Be there in one five minutes. Can you throw smoke?"

"Roger, the smoke."

"We have an aircraft inbound now."

"THREE SEVEN. You up for a Medevac?" asked Rice.

Newhawser glanced up at the greenhouse above his head and rolled his eyes. That was the disadvantage of flying trail. A follow on mission came up and it was always passed on to trail. Most times no one volunteered to take trail's place because it was normally a hassle. Everyone else shut down, slept, read, played cards, while Trail was out flying in the war.

"Roger. I'll take it."

"It's an emergency," said a voice that had to be Fallon's. Rice would never remind him of something he could figure out himself.

"Roger." Newhawser glanced out the cargo compartment door and saw the door gunner returning the nozzle to the post. It meant they, too, had heard the message.

As soon as they were on board, Newhawser called the tower, asked for a scramble departure to the north and was cleared out from the refueling pad. Newhawser picked up to a hover, slipped to the right, away from the rest of the flight, and then turned. He eased to the right again so that he was clear of the other helicopters and then dumped the nose for a few feet before climbing out to the north, over the edge of the perimeter that looked out into a low-lying swampy area.

Once clear of the Cu Chi traffic pattern, he turned toward the west and headed out. The Song Sai Gon was on his right and as the base camp slipped away behind him, he passed Trung Lap, famous for its Inter-Paddy Airport.

As soon as he saw Can Me To in the distance, he was on the radio. "Zulu six, this is Hornet three seven. Say condition of LZ."

"Lima Zulu is cold."

"Roger, cold. Can you throw smoke?"

There was a delay and then a cloud of yellow began to billow up through a huge hole in the trees.

"There," said Stockton pointing.

"I see it," said Newhawser. "Everyone ready?"

"All set."

Newhawser squeezed the mike button again. "ID yellow."

"Roger, yellow. We have you in sight."

Newhawser watched the smoke drifting, saw that the winds around the LZ matched those reported at Cu Chi and broke to the south so that he could land to the north. As he passed the LZ, he looked into it and saw that it was oval, with the long axis east and west, but the difference between that diameter and the one of the north-south line didn't seem to be significant.

He dropped down toward tops of the trees, keeping the LZ in sight. In flight school they talked about circling the LZ, studying the terrain and planning an approach that would take advantage of the long axis, the winds and the terrain. In Vietnam, if you were in sight for ten seconds, the VC could shoot your ass out of the air. Newhawser glanced, saw as much as he could and then disappeared to the south. A klick away, he turned, used the smoke as a guide and raced back, no more than fifteen feet above the trees.

They came up on the LZ and as they did, Newhawser rolled over to the right, kicked the pedals and then sucked in an armload of pitch. The helicopter rolled up on the right and the rotors bit the air, slowing them. As they began to sink toward the ground, right side down, Newhawser kicked the pedals again, whipped the cyclic around and lowered the collective. They dropped toward the ground with the skids now under them. Using the collective to adjust the rate of descent, he touched down.

As they landed, three soldiers ran at them carrying a figure in a poncho liner. One of them leaped up into the cargo compartment. He lifted as the other men pushed, and they rolled the wounded man onto the deck.

"Go!" yelled the man.

The two who had helped, turned and ran off. Newhawser turned, saw one mud-splattered man and another covered with blood and looking pale.

Newhawser pulled pitch, came up to a hover and dumped the nose. He charged the tree line and then popped up over it. As soon as they were clear of the treetops, he turned to the east and dropped back toward the ground. He didn't bother to gain any altitude. He held at three hundred feet and the airspeed at one hundred and twenty knots.

In moments they were close to Cu Chi. Newhawser began a rapid climb, and as he did he called the tower, requesting an approach to the Twelfth Evac.

"Roger. Can you hold?"

"Negative. I have a wounded soldier."

"Hornet seven six seven, you are cleared straight in to the Twelfth Evac. Call your break."

"Inbound now."

"Roger."

Newhawser saw the pad. Stockton reached for the Fox Mike, turning it to six two decimal five. When the tuning squeal faded, he said, "Ah, this is Hornet three seven alpha inbound with a wounded man on board."

"Say nature of the wounds," came the immediate reply.

Stockton looked over the back of his seat. "To the legs. Shrapnel."

"Roger. We'll meet you on the pad."

"On final now," said Stockton.

Over the intercom Newhawser said, "How's it look back there, Jonesy?"

"Guy's in pain and awake. Looks pale, but I think he's going to be fine."

Newhawser shot his approach to the corner of the Twelfth Evac's pad that bordered the dirt road. As they hovered there, a cloud of dust swirled up, surrounding them. Through the dust, Newhawser saw the double doors of the hospital snap open and three people, two of them pushing a gurney, come running toward them. Newhawser dropped the collective and the aircraft settled to the ground, the dust and dirt blowing away from them.

As the medics dragged the wounded soldier from the cargo compartment, the radio crackled. "Trail, say location."

"Twelfth Evac."

"Roger. Join the flight at POL, ASAP."

"Roger."

"Now what?" asked Stockton.

"Who knows?" said Newhawser as he picked up to a hover, turning so that they could take off. "Who knows?"

As soon as the helicopter had taken off, Fetterman moved the men from the LZ back into the trees. They spread out in a rough circle for security and waited.

Gerber approached and said, "I'm calling this off. We'll fall back to the village, and Kepler can talk to the locals before pickup."

"Enemy might still be near," cautioned Fetterman.

"But more probably he scattered more booby traps or maybe left a sniper or two. More of our people hurt and no real chance of catching them."

"Yes, sir," said Fetterman.

"You don't agree?"

Fetterman shrugged. "I would guess that even if we found the enemy, it wouldn't be the ones we want. A cover team but not the assassination squad."

"We're doing no good here. It took us too long to get into the field and too long to get into the jungle. We announced the arrival with helicopters. I can't see continuing unless we found something to suggest that we are on the right track."

"Want me to take the point?" asked Fetterman.

"If you don't mind."

Fetterman nodded and moved toward the east. He stopped in the shade of a dwarf tree, crouching on the hard-packed earth. He touched his face with his hand and then wiped the sweat on the thigh of his jungle fatigues. Without speaking, he sent two men off as flankers and then moved out himself, taking the point.

In a matter of minutes they were moving through the light forest again. The trees were only fifteen, twenty feet tall, with small leaves that faced the sun. The light filtered through easily, making the march hot. The humidity didn't help. Uniforms turned black with sweat that never dried. The men moved slower now, taking it easy. They were alert, but not tense. They had already been in the village and knew what to expect there.

In an hour they were back at the edge of the jungle, watching the village from hiding. The locals had not yet gone into the fields for the day. The rice paddies were unattended and the oxen were still tied to the posts. A few people moved around outside, many of them youngsters who didn't understand war or danger and who believed they would live forever. The adults stayed inside, except for one old man who prowled the ruins of the school building. He was carefully separating the broken cinder blocks from those that could be reused.

Fetterman decided that the enemy hadn't returned, because everything looked so suspicious. If there was an ambush waiting in the village, everything would have looked peaceful, and all the inhabitants would be outside working, as if nothing was wrong and the VC weren't close.

As the Americans moved out of the forest, the few people around fled. The old man sat down in the middle of the school and refused to move or speak. He was waiting for the Americans to leave so that he could get back to work.

The body of the school-teacher still lay where it had fallen. Fetterman moved toward it and looked down, shaking his head. He took his poncho liner and covered the dead woman.

"Let's get the choppers in here," said Gerber approaching him.

"What about her?"

"Let the Vietnamese worry about it. Once we're clear and they realize the NVA are gone, they'll bury her. That's the best thing."

"I don't like that, sir," said Fetterman. "She was a teacher. All she wanted to do was teach the children so that their lives would be a little better."

"How do you know?" asked Gerber.

"I don't. I just remember my teachers. Most of them had no politics. They were dedicated people who were never rewarded for their hard work, who were underpaid and occasionally despised, and yet they were there every morning ready for another day of it.''

"Tony, it's best if we leave the body. It'll be a reminder to these people."

"Yes, sir, but I'm not sure of the message."

Kepler came over. He held his weapon in his left hand and there was sweat on his face, dripping onto his collar. "Locals refuse to talk. Hell, they refuse to come out."

"I can't blame them," said Fetterman.

"Let's get everyone to the eastern side of the village and get the choppers in here," said Gerber.

Kepler looked at his watch. "We've blown the whole morning and haven't learned a damned thing."

"And we've had one man wounded," said Gerber. "We've got to think this thing through."

"And react faster," said Fetterman.

"Exactly."

9

WEST OF CAN ME TO

They knew the Americans were close. The choppers had told them the Americans were coming, and it was only a matter of time before they arrived. Nhu hoped that it would be a big victory, one that would be talked about for years to come. The all-powerful Americans walking into an ambush and being massacred. That was what he hoped.

As the sound of the choppers faded, meaning that the enemy was now on the ground, Nhu felt the excitement burn through him. The Americans would know which way the NVA had gone because they made no effort to hide the trail. All Nhu and his friends had to do was remain patient. The enemy would come to them.

But then they had stumbled over the booby trap. Nhu heard the explosion and knew what it meant. The Americans would hold up, help their wounded comrade before continuing on. They could be counted on to do that. The simplest way to stop a pursuit was to wound, not kill, one or two of the enemy.

He listened as a single chopper approached, landed and took off, wondering why they didn't move forward to try to shoot it down. A single helicopter could easily be downed, and then all of them could be out of the way before the other helicopters could be summoned.

But none of that happened. They sat where they were, waiting until it was obvious that the Americans had turned around again, heading back to the village. Until it was obvious that they had been distracted.

The squad remained where it was, concealed in the bushes of the forest, listening to the sounds of the jungle around them. The inactivity was becoming a strain.

But then Van broke cover, moving from the shadows and out onto the pathway. He stood there for a moment in his sweat-soaked black pajamas, letting the rest of the men see him, and then waved a hand once. As he did, the rest of the men began to move from hiding.

Nhu hesitated for a moment, taking a drink from his canteen. He poured some of the water into his hand and splashed it up on his face. Cooled slightly, he capped his canteen and moved out of hiding to join the others.

Van pointed to one man who ran off to take the point. Van indicated two others and they dropped off as the rear guard. They moved out, sticking to the cover provided by the forest. In the distance to the east was the sound of helicopters. It meant that Van's decision to get out was the right one. No one would be coming at them.

AT HOTEL THREE, Gerber had dismissed the grunts, thanking them for their help. They were told their friend was at the Twelfth Evac Hospital at Cu Chi and that he'd probably be sent to Japan to recover in a week or so. The pilots were told to refuel their aircraft and then to move them to the tarmac pad in front of the SOG building. It was next to the Air America pad, distinguished by the silver-and-white C-47s parked on it most of the time.

Back at the SOG building, Gerber, Kepler and Fetterman sat around the briefing room, studying some maps spread out before them on a table. Each man had a can of Coke in front of him.

Gerber had unbuckled his pistol belt and shucked off his pack, which now lay on the floor near his feet. His fatigues were sweat-stained under the arms, down the back and under the places where his ruck and his pistol belt had been. His M-16 sat on the table. He picked up his Coke, took a drink and then asked, "You know what was wrong with the mission this morning?"

"We were late getting started," said Fetterman. "We should have been airborne last night, the instant the message came in to us."

"Close," said Gerber. "Very close, but I'm not sure even that would've been enough. Take us an hour to respond, even if we were sitting on the aircraft waiting."

"An hour might do it," said Fetterman.

"It might," agreed Gerber, "but that's not the problem. What's happened here is that we've let the NVA take the initiative. We wait for them to act and then respond to it. They don't act and we sit around waiting."

Kepler pulled the map closer to him. He looked at the wide open spaces between Saigon and the Cambodian border. Dozens of tiny villages so small that no one had bothered to mark them on the map or give them names. Just a reference to numerous hamlets and a scattering of black dots in the approximate locations. And there were hundreds, thousands of places for the enemy to hide. Hell, with the situation the way it was, they didn't even have to hide. They could strip their military gear and claim to be farmers. With the proper ID, they'd get away with it, and the NVA all had the proper ID.

"There's no way that we can gain the initiative," said Kepler looking up from the map. "Just no fucking way to gain the initiative."

"Derek, that's leg thinking." Gerber took a swallow of his Coke. "We've got to think of a way to take the initiative away from them."

"One obvious way," said Fetterman, "is for Derek's agents to start snooping around to see if we can pinpoint the location of the squad. Either find their base camp or find out where they are going to be."

Gerber looked at the Intelligence NCO. "And you need to get with the G-2 pukes over at MACV. See if you can pinpoint the locations of the other attacks. Put them on the map and see if that gives us a clue."

"Yes, sir."

Gerber turned his attention to Fetterman. "Now, if we keep the men and the aircraft airborne all the time, we'll tire everyone out and not be ready. Keeping them on the ground waiting isn't the answer either."

Fetterman nodded. "If Derek's search produces anything, then we could patrol the zone."

"I can't see that producing any results. We almost need to use the aircraft. A ground search is too slow to produce any results."

"So we patrol from the air," said Fetterman. "We see something and we can swoop in on it."

"That might work," said Gerber. He held up a hand and then added, "One ship as C and C and the other four filled with troops."

"Something like that," said Fetterman.

"Okay, I'll meet with Fallon and see what he needs. Tony, you coordinate the Mike Force. I want two complete detachments. One to rest while the other is working. That way we'll be ready twenty-four hours a day."

"What about the pilots? You're going to wear them out in no time," said Kepler.

"Again, I'll get with Fallon and see what he has to say."
Gerber looked at the two sergeants. "That about cover everything?"

Fetterman nodded and Kepler said, "I'll head on over to
MACV to see what I can learn."

From outside came the sound of helicopters approaching.
First they were no louder than the aircraft operating at Tan Son
Nhut, but then the roar of the turbines and the popping of the
blades washed over the building making conversation almost
impossible. The tin on the roof rattled in the turbulence.

Gerber glanced toward the front of the building and
shouted, "Let's do it."

Both Fetterman and Kepler got up and left. Gerber sat there
for a moment, finished his Coke and then followed the NCOs.
He reached the front of the building and stopped near the
door. The sound from outside had faded slightly and the
building didn't seem about to blow away. He hesitated there
and then opened the door.

The five helicopters sat on the tarmac in front of the building, the noses facing the door. Gerber could see the pilots sitting behind the Plexiglas and realized what good targets they
were. Sitting in a hot LZ, unable to fire at the enemy, their
heads and chests exposed to enemy bullets while waiting for
the men to either leap from the rear or climb back on. And if
they were struggling with wounded men, it could seem like
hours for the pilots. He decided that he'd never say another
nasty thing about the kids who flew the choppers.

As the whine of the turbines died and the rotors slowed, the
pilots began to get out. They moved toward the center, standing near the nose of one of the helicopters. Gerber left the
building, stepping into the heat and humidity of the late
morning.

Fallon saw him and asked, "What's the plan for the rest of
the day?"

"That's a good question," said Gerber. "I don't want your people to get too far afield here, but then, without the strikers in place, there isn't much for them to do."

"Why not let us get set up in the VOQ?" said one of the pilots.

"Fine," said Gerber. He thought for a moment. "When you get finished there, come back over here and we'll set the ground rules."

"Fine," said Fallon.

"And Captain, why don't you come with me. I've got a couple of ideas about this operation that I need to discuss with you."

"Sir," said one of the pilots, stepping forward. "If you're going to be talking about tactics, I think you'd better have one of the ACs in on it."

Gerber looked at him and then at Fallon.

"It would be a good idea," said Fallon.

"All right, Mr. . . . ."

"Rice, sir."

"Rice. You come on in with us."

Fallon turned and said, "Mr. Newhawser, you'll be in charge of this."

"Great," said Newhawser. "My first command. All right, men, listen up."

"Take charge somewhere else," said Fallon. "And I want everyone back here within an hour."

The group began to break up. Gerber, along with Rice and Fallon headed back into the SOG building. Rice opened the door, let both Gerber and Fallon in first, then followed them. They walked down the hall and into the briefing room.

Before they sat down, Rice asked, "There any place to get a Coke?"

"Refrigerator in the dayroom. Drop some money into the can so that we can resupply it."

"Certainly," said Rice.

Fallon dug into his pocket and brought out an MPC dollar. "I'll pay if you'll get them."

Rice snatched the bill, snapped it once and disappeared. When he was gone, Gerber said, "I'm not clear on your chain of command."

"It's a bizarre system," said Fallon. "I outrank all of them, but don't have the flight time to qualify as an aircraft commander. Therefore, Rice, as the AC, outranks me in the air."

"So who gives final approval to the plan?"

Fallon dropped into the nearest chair. "I'll approve it, on the condition that Rice accepts it too. His major concern will be the capabilities of the aircraft and our ability to meet the mission requirements. He'll know what can't be done, and that means physically can't be done because of the limitations of the helicopters."

Rice returned, put one of the Cokes in front of Fallon, handed one to Gerber and then sat down, opening his own. "Couldn't see leaving you out, sir."

"Thank you." Gerber opened his and took a drink, thinking he was going to float away if he wasn't careful. He pointed to the map and said, "I don't know what all you've been told about the assignment here."

"Not much," said Fallon.

"Then here's the story." Gerber used the map to tell them about the assassination squad and their terrorist operations. He gave them as much information as he could and then finished by saying that their assignment was to eliminate the squad. That was why the helicopters had been assigned to them.

"Then we just wait for them to attack somewhere and swoop in on them," said Fallon.

"I'd rather not wait," said Gerber. "What I'd like to do is search for them, find them and eliminate them."

Rice took a deep drink, belched, then hunched over the map. "There's an awful lot of territory to cover. Especially with the limited resources you have."

"I know," said Gerber. "I need your advice."

"Ground patrols?" asked Fallon.

"Of limited value."

Rice sat back and said, "We could use our helicopters. One as the command and control, or maybe more of a scout, and the other four with troops, standing off. Then, if something is spotted, we can put them down to check it out."

"Could we operate with another scout?" asked Gerber.

"Hell, they could all be scouts," said Rice, "but then you've got no real reaction force. We have two scouts and three aircraft with troops, you'd have to deploy everyone at once. If the second scout found something, you wouldn't have people to cover it."

Gerber nodded. "And a single ship of grunts isn't all that much."

"What, seven, eight guys," said Rice. "We drop them into an NVA platoon and it'd be over before it started."

"So you'd recommend one scout and four reaction ships?" said Gerber.

Rice looked at Fallon and then at Gerber. He realized that Gerber was addressing him, not Fallon. "Yes, sir. That way the men going in would have half a chance to survive. We find anything more than a platoon and we're going to be able to tell that from the air."

"How would you run this?" asked Gerber.

"Depending on the location of the scout, I'd have the grunts on the ground with the aircraft, maybe at flight idle, waiting to hear something from the scout. We move into the Hobo or Boi Loi Woods and I'd have the flight standing by at Trung Lap or Dau Tieng. Cu Chi is too busy. Dau Tieng has refueling but Trung Lap doesn't."

"Would it make any sense to get a truck out there?" asked Gerber.

"For refueling? Not really. Cu Chi is five minutes away," responded Rice.

"How many troops can you carry?"

Rice shrugged. "Depends. If you're talking about grunts with full packs. Six. You talking about men and ammo and no other heavy equipment. Seven or eight. Vietnamese strikers. Ten. If we had H models, you could cram a few more in."

"Then you have what?"

"All D models. D for dogs. The humidity gets to them. Weakens them."

"Captain Fallon," said Gerber.

"I can't fault what Mr. Rice is telling you."

"Okay, then. How soon can you be ready to implement the plan?"

"How soon can you get your strikers here?" asked Rice.

"That soon?"

"Yes, sir," said Rice. "That soon."

MORROW SAT IN THE ROOM with the rest of the reporters, sipping coffee and eating rolls that had been supplied for them. She didn't bother talking to any of the others because she didn't feel like it. The depression that had wrapped her the day before had returned, and even the thoughts of Gerber's words were not enough to kill it now.

But then the briefing officer entered and stepped to the center of the room, pushing her depression aside. He was a young man, a first lieutenant who had pale skin and dark hair. He looked and acted nervous, sweat staining his pressed and starched jungle fatigues even in the air-conditioning of the MACV briefing room.

He set his notes on the lectern in front of him, cleared his throat in an attempt to get the attention of the reporters who had chosen to ignore him. When that failed, he held up his hands and said, "Please."

Only a few of the reporters fell silent. The lieutenant glanced to the right, where an NCO stood, but the man was no help. The sergeant only grinned and shrugged. Finally the lieutenant yelled, "If you'll take your seats we can get this show over with."

For a moment it seemed that no one cared to get the show on the road, and then reluctantly they took their seats and the noise faded.

"I have a brief statement to make. Last night Vietcong terrorists entered the small village of Can Me To, destroyed the school building and then murdered the teacher when she refused to teach their manifestos rather than the established courses. Finished with their heinous crimes, they fled into the night. Patrols by American soldiers have been unable to find a trace of the enemy soldiers."

He folded his notes and then looked up. "I will entertain some questions now."

Morrow stood up. "When were the soldiers sent into the field?"

"This morning. After dawn."

"A little late, wasn't it?" asked another reporter.

"The troops were dispatched as quickly as possible. In this case, it meant a slight delay."

"Delay?" yelled a man. "That's what? Ten or twelve hours? What did they expect to find?"

"There have been no reports from the soldiers."

"But the VC would be long gone."

"That would be an . . . accurate prediction," said the lieutenant. "Steps are being taken to remedy that situation."

"What does that mean?"

The lieutenant suddenly realized that he was saying more than he was supposed to. He grinned sheepishly. "It means simply that we're looking for the enemy."

Two men were up and shouting. One voice boomed out, drowning the other. "Is there a concentrated effort to find these terrorists?"

The lieutenant again looked at the NCO for help, but there was none offered. He shrugged. "All I know is that we put a patrol into the field to find the enemy. No contact has been reported."

There were more shouted questions. Reporters were screaming at the lieutenant who didn't know what to do. He'd walked out to make a simple statement and found himself grilled by the reporters who needed a story. When they became so concerned with a single death in a war zone, it meant there was little else going on. The lieutenant noticed that not one of the reporters asked for permission to visit the village and explore the questions for themselves.

"Gentlemen," he shouted, and then noticed Morrow. "And ladies. Please."

But the shouting continued. They were like jackals on the scent of death. They wouldn't let go, yelling questions that the lieutenant now refused to answer. He tried to silence them again, but couldn't do it. When the NCO refused to help him, he fled from the room, closing the door behind him.

As the door slammed, one of the reporters shouted, "Just what in the hell are you trying to hide?"

The lieutenant knew that the reporter would never accept the real answer that the military was not trying to hide anything. And he could think of nothing that would satisfy them. His only recourse had been to get out before he let the information about the scattered missions and the assassination squad drop.

10

THE CARASEL HOTEL
SAIGON

Gerber sat in front of the air conditioner rattling under the window, the cool air blowing out at him. He had taken off his jungle fatigue jacket and dropped it on the floor. He'd then gone to the wardrobe, opened it and taken out the bottle of bourbon. He'd taken a long pull as he walked into the bathroom and picked up a glass, splashing some of the liquor into it. He held it up, as if examining it, and then drank deeply.

Back in his room, he sat down on the only chair and propped his feet up on the window sill. He was tired from a night of planning a mission that succeeded only in wounding one man and accomplishing nothing else. A thrown-together mission that was half a day too late to do anything.

But the afternoon had been better. The pilots had helped him design a mission that might work. Kepler had retrieved the information they wanted, bringing it to the SOG building and plotting it on an overlay that was unclassified when it was pulled off the map. It had been some help. It had given them an area to search that was much smaller than what they originally had.

And Fetterman had managed to get a company of Nung strikers assigned to them at Tan Son Nhut. They'd brought everything they needed, including tents which had been pitched on the open ground behind the SOG building. They were far enough away from the flight line to please the Air Force. Fetterman had decided to spend the night there so that the Air Police didn't worry about the strikers. Kepler was with him.

Gerber finished his drink, stood up and stretched. He felt a bit wobbly. Another day's delay. It had been late when the strikers arrived. Kepler had also arrived late, too late to begin that night. An air search would do no good after dark unless they were equipped with Firefly—and they weren't. Besides, Firefly only found the enemy, not a specific unit.

Reluctantly Gerber had released the pilots, telling them that nothing would happen until morning. They were free until zero six hundred the next day. He'd expect them to be at their aircraft then, ready to go, but until then, he didn't care what they did. The night belonged to them.

Leaving Fetterman and Kepler with the strikers, Gerber had taken a taxi back to the hotel. He would relax for one more night and then put his plan into operation. Once it was in motion, he expected to stay with it until the NVA were killed, captured or driven from his AO.

Gerber turned to the window and looked out onto Saigon. The streets at dusk were filled with people. But then, the streets always were filled with people. There was a tone to the city that was not shared by other urban areas in the world. The people lived at a frenzied pace, as if they knew the situation would change soon and it would be for the worse. Their lives, their environment, their culture was something extremely fragile that they wanted to savor while they could. In a day it could be gone.

Gerber stepped to the wardrobe to get his bottle of bourbon. He filled the glass again and then sat down. He didn't bother with the room light, letting the neon glow filter in from the street. Saigon was definitely a strange place, unique in the world.

Sometimes it was a depressing city with the rows of beggars, their arms or legs lost in the war. Sometimes it was a joyous city, as they celebrated their attempts to move into the twentieth century. It wasn't a city he could look at and not feel something, whether it was anger for the people who wanted someone else to do everything for them, or a sorrow for what would happen if the war was lost.

The knock at the door startled him. He jumped, then opened the door and found the hallway vacant. Stepping out, he saw Morrow walking toward the elevator.

"Hey! Robin!" he called.

She stopped and turned. "Mack, I figured you'd still be gone."

"Well, you have to give me a chance to answer the door before you decide to run away."

She came back to him and stopped, looking around. Seeing no one watching them, she kissed him. "That's for last night."

He turned, pulling her into his arms. "We didn't get a chance to do anything last night."

"We didn't have to," she told him. "The talking was enough. I tried to let it get to me again this morning, and it worked for an hour or so, but then, suddenly, I knew you were absolutely right. There was no sense in worrying about my sister. Let her have her few moments of glory, because she's not going to have many of them."

Gerber pushed the door closed and turned on the light. "You want a drink?"

"Hell, no! That's the last thing I want." She walked to the air conditioner and turned it off. "It's getting too cold in here."

"Too cold for what?"

She reached around behind her and unhooked the top of her dress. She inched the zipper down and shrugged her shoulders, letting the garment fall away so that it was bunched around her waist. She pushed it over her hips and let it pool at her feet. She was standing in front of him in her bra and panties, her perspiration highlighting her body. Without waiting for him to speak or to react, she unfastened her bra and let it drop to the floor.

"This give you a clue?" she asked, her voice quiet, almost purring.

"Yeah, it does." He grinned broadly. "But I thought we should get something to eat."

She didn't let that bother her. Instead she hooked her thumbs into the waistband of her black bikini panties and rolled them down her thighs so that she was standing naked in front of him.

"You sure you still want to eat?"

"Of course," said Gerber. "But not right now." He moved toward her, and took her in his arms, aware of the shapes and textures of her body. "Not right now," he repeated.

NEWHAWSER SAT IN THE dayroom area of the VOQ, looking at the small black-and-white television which was showing him a *Star Trek* rerun. It was the same show that had been on the night before, but then he hadn't been around to see it the night before. And it made no difference that he had seen the same episode nearly a year earlier while in flight school. Back in the World, every Friday night a group of the WOCs watched *The Wild Wild West* on CBS and then switched over to NBC for *Star Trek*. It was cheaper than dating the local girls, who were only interested in how much money they could get the GIs to spend on them. Besides, they couldn't legally drink off base because they were all under twenty-one, and even if they could have they would have had to drive quite a distance since all the counties around Fort Rucker, Alabama were dry.

Lee Hoskinson and Sam Rice entered and sat down on the old faded couch shoved against one wall. "*Star Trek*, again, huh?" said Rice.

"Yeah."

"They ever get that security problem worked out?" he asked with a straight face.

Newhawser shook his head. "Nope. Kirk and the boys just beamed down with two more security men. Neither security guy survived the trip."

"Got to be the world's worst assignment," said Rice. "Join the *Enterprise* security team and die before the show is over. Can't believe they get anyone to beam down with them."

"But more importantly," said Newhawser, "you up for a trip downtown? Tu Do Street and the honky-tonks?"

"After last night," said Hoskinson, "you want to go downtown?"

"I've been in Vietnam for damned near a year and I've been to Saigon twice. Once to fly out for R and R and the other time down to Cholon to buy steaks for a unit party."

"You get the steaks?" asked Hoskinson.

"Of course." He glanced at the screen as Kirk and the boys were beaming back to the ship. "Anyway, I'm for going downtown, finding a steak and checking out Tu Do Street."

"You know, if you catch a disease they can hold up your DEROS for a couple of weeks."

"Christ, I didn't say anything about jumping some bimbo. I just want to see Tu Do street. We grab a cab, head down and look it over."

"And we'll be back by midnight?" asked Hoskinson.

Newhawser rolled his eyes. "Midnight. One o'clock. We'll be back before takeoff tomorrow."

Rice clapped his hands. "Let's do it then. I'll let Fallon know that we're going downtown."

"Make sure you tell him we're going and don't ask permission. You ask and he can say no. You just assume that we're going without having to ask and he'll go with the flow."

As Rice headed back down the hall, Newhawser turned off the TV and then walked to the door with Hoskinson following. He stepped onto the porch and looked down at the street. A couple of jeeps, a truck, but no sign of a cab.

"Guess we'll have to walk out to the front gate to catch a cab."

They stood waiting until Rice appeared, dragging Logan and Stockton with him. "Found these youngsters lounging around and figured they should see the sights of Saigon before we all get killed."

"You shouldn't talk like that," said Newhawser seriously.

"Why not?"

Newhawser took a deep breath and then rubbed his face as if nervous. "Dan Mitchell talked like that . . ."

Logan waited and then said, "Talked like what?"

"Made jokes about buying the farm. Made jokes about crashing and burning and being afraid of others crashing and throwing broken parts on his airplane."

"And?"

"He got killed. Crashed and burned and threw parts on my airplane. You shouldn't joke about that."

"Bullshit," said Stockton.

Logan looked at Stockton and then at Newhawser and realized that it was, indeed, bullshit.

"You see?" said Rice. "You see? These new guys don't know enough to save themselves. They have to go downtown."

"But if we take them," said Hoskinson, "who'll preflight the aircraft tomorrow?"

"Fuck 'em," said Newhawser. "They'll just have to be ready to do it."

They started off then, walking toward the gate. As they neared it, a multicolored taxi, red, blue and yellow, dived out of the military traffic and honked at them. Rice raised his hand and the cab stopped.

"You ride, GI?"

Stockton grabbed the door handle and yelled, "Shotgun."

"Fucking new guys," mumbled Hoskinson. "Don't even know enough to want to ride in the back." He opened the rear door and then took a step back. "What the fuck died in here?"

"You ride, GI?" repeated the driver.

"Fucker's got a one track mind."

Rice pushed by and said, "I'm not going to stand around out here waiting." He climbed in. "Tu Do Street."

Newhawser joined him. Hoskinson finally got in as Logan squeezed in the front with Stockton.

The driver waited for the door to close and then spun the wheel, pulling into traffic. He didn't wait for a gap, he just pulled out. There was a squeal of tires and the blare of a horn, but he didn't notice.

They slowed at the gate so that the guard could see who was inside. He waved them through. They entered the traffic whipping from side to side. There were angry shouts that the driver didn't seem to hear.

The traffic was thick, even at dusk. Cars and jeeps and trucks and lambrettas and pedicabs. There were pedestrians swarming along the streets. Thousands of people outside, down on the street, looking for something to do, something that would last.

They then turned down a side street, entered another and finally pulled into a third that was brightly lighted. Music from the bars drifted into the street, adding a new dimension to the noise. Gone was the rumble of engines, replaced by the rumble of drums. The honking of horns was drowned by electric guitars and the screaming of rock and roll bands.

"Yeah," yelled Newhawser beating on the back of the seat. "This is it. Let us out now."

The driver yanked on the wheel, peeled across two lanes of traffic and hit the curb.

"Five thousand P," he said.

"Christ, fifty bucks for a fifteen minute cab ride?" said Rice. "Absolutely no fucking way."

"You pay five thousand P."

"Stockton, give the little asshole five bucks and we're out of here."

"One thousand P," said the driver with no less enthusiasm.

Stockton took out a ten dollar MPC bill and the driver grabbed, stuffing it into his shirt. "One thousand P plus tip," he said.

"Fuck him," said Rice, throwing open the door. He stepped onto the sidewalk and watched as a Vietnamese woman walked by wearing the shortest skirt he'd ever seen. As Newhawser joined him, Rice pointed. "If she didn't look to be twelve, I'd jump her right here."

"You'd jump anything in a skirt who didn't look twelve, given half a chance. But then, look is the operative word here. She could *be* twelve, as long as she didn't look it."

The others crowded around them on the sidewalk. Logan looked at the neon blinking brightly in the window near them. "Where we going?"

Newhawser stepped to the door and yanked it open. A blast of rock and roll washed out. The humid air of the bar, smelling of *ba muoi ba* and vomit boiled out.

"Yeah," yelled Rice over the noise. "This is the place. Got to be."

They pushed their way in, around the crowd of GIs in sweat-soaked civilian clothes. A few old NCOs, still in jungle fatigues, sat at a table near a small raised stage where a Vietnamese girl danced naked, her body glistening in the revolving spotlights.

"Christ, it's hot," said Stockton. His shirt was already wet, and his hair hung down, looking as if it had been washed a moment earlier.

"Table," yelled Hoskinson, pushing through the crowd. He reached it the same time as another man. Both sat down glaring at one another.

Newhawser approached, and over the driving beat of the rock and roll, heard the man announce, "I'm a staff sergeant, so you'd better get your ass out of here."

Newhawser shook his head. Had to be some asshole clerk from MACV who thought rank was important and didn't realize that everyone there outranked him anyway.

"Why don't you haul ass before you get hurt, Sarge."

Two others joined the man and said, "Why don't you?"

Newhawser grinned and then said, "Nope. Too early in the evening for a fight."

"You're giving up?" asked the staff sergeant.

"Nope. You are." He pointed at Stockton, Logan and Rice. "Got you outnumbered."

The staff sergeant looked at the others and then abandoned the table. The other pilots sat down. "Now," yelled Rice, over the shouting GIs, the screaming Vietnamese and the rock and roll, "one of you peter pilots go buy us some beer."

Stockton waited, but Logan didn't move. "Hell, I've got it," he said.

"Now," said Newhawser, "we can stay here and look for women, or just hang out and then go look for food."

Before anyone could answer, the girl on the stage stopped dancing and disappeared into the back. She was replaced by another girl, fully dressed. She walked onto the stage, began dancing in time to music that only she heard and in ten seconds was as naked as the first girl.

"Oh, yeah," yelled Rice. "Oh yeah."

Newhawser took a deep breath and nearly choked. The air was thick with cigarette smoke. A blue haze hovered in the few lights. It looked as if the place was on fire but the show was so good that no one wanted to leave.

On a stool at the end of the bar, a GI sat with a Vietnamese girl. He had one hand in her blouse and the other up her skirt. She was swaying in time to his movements. Newhawser slapped Rice on the arm and pointed. He leaned in close and shouted, "Least he could do is find a room."

"Why? She doesn't care."

Stockton reappeared and put the beer on the table in front of each of the other pilots. As he sat down, he shouted, "They made me buy the bottles."

"That's so you don't break them," yelled Newhawser. "Bottles are hard to get."

A Vietnamese girl walked by and Rice snagged her around the thighs, pulling her close. She wore a white blouse so wet that they could see through it. Her long hair was sweat-damp. She grinned at Rice and fell into his lap.

"Hi, GI. You want short-time."

Rice slipped his hand along her sweat-damp thigh and said, "You bet."

"You come with me," she said.

"Yes," said Rice standing up.

Another man appeared and said, "The lady was with me."

"Oh, Christ," said Newhawser, "now we're going to get into a fight over a whore."

Rice however, wasn't interested in a fight. He kissed the woman and said, "Next time, baby."

"GI yellow."

"No, I just fight Communists, not Americans."

"A wise move," said the man.

Rice started to respond and then shrugged. "Whatever."

"Fucking coward," said the man.

Newhawser stood up then and said, "You just couldn't leave it alone, could you? Had to keep pushing it." He then stomped on the man's toes and hit him in the face. The man fell to the floor.

Rice glanced up and laughed. "Let's get out of here now." He leaped to his feet and pushed his way through to the door. Three of the others followed, but Newhawser stood his ground, looking at the man on the floor.

"Let's go," yelled Rice.

Newhawser looked down at the man who hadn't moved. He backed up, like the rear guard protecting his fellows. The shouting of the GIs hadn't changed, the girl on the stage hadn't seen a thing, and no one seemed to care about the brief fight anyway.

On the street, Rice was laughing so hard that he was doubled over. No one else thought it was that funny. Newhawser wiped the sweat from his face and realized that for the first time in Vietnam, it seemed cool outside. That was the difference between the temperature in the bar and that outside.

Rice finally stood up and asked, "Now what? Food?"

"We'd better do something before Newhawser gets us into a fight and we end up in jail again," said Hoskinson.

"Let's get a cab," said Newhawser. "And we'll find some food."

"Good," said Stockton. "And then we can go back to Tan Son Nhut. So that we don't get into more trouble."

Now Newhawser laughed. "Well, I've seen Tu Do Street."

"That you have," said Rice. "That you have."

11

TAN SON NHUT

Gerber turned on the lights in the dayroom area of the SOG building and then went in search of coffee. He found a pot in the radio room where two men monitored various UHF, VHF and FM equipment. It was a dark room with code books sitting on the desks in front of them, and where tiny red, green and amber lights blazed and needles on vu-meters danced. There were occasional bursts of static, the result of a thunderstorm somewhere over South Vietnam.

"Anything interesting coming in?" asked Gerber as he filled a Styrofoam cup with the steaming black liquid.

One of the sergeants turned and looked at him and shook his head. "Pretty quiet night."

"Figures," said Gerber. He took the coffee and left, crossing the hall to the briefing room. He flipped on the lights and then blinked in the sudden brightness of the fluorescent tubes. Sipping the coffee, he walked to the maps on the wall and studied one of them. It showed the area around Cu Chi, the Hobo Woods, Nui Ba Den and Dau Tieng. There was nothing on it to excite him. A flat representation of what was west of Saigon. Open ground, forest, light jungle and rubber plantations. A thousand places for the enemy to hide and no clue about where to look for them.

He finished the coffee and threw the cup into the wastebasket near the door. Turning off the lights, he walked back to the front door and stood there for a moment. Finally he opened it and stepped out into the muggy heat of the night. The lights from the runway bled over the airfield. The five helicopters stood where they had been parked the day before, the blades tied down and the cargo compartment doors shut. The M-60s had been removed from the pussy mounts and stored inside, out of sight under the troop seats.

One of the crew chiefs appeared, opened a door and began getting the ship ready for flight. Gerber watched him for a moment as he removed the protective covers from the Pitot tube and rear of the turbine, and then walked to the side of the building. Spread out on the open field across the blacktopped street were the tents erected by the strikers. Guards were walking the perimeter of the camp, but they were more for show than for protection. A Vietcong or NVA attack on Tan Son Nhut would be detected long before they could get to the tent city.

Gerber walked across the street and was challenged by one of the guards who demanded that he halt and identify himself. The man spoke heavily accented English.

"Gerber, Captain. Looking for Sergeant Fetterman."

"Advance, Gerber, and be recognized."

Behind the guard, Gerber saw the shape of Fetterman materialize.

"Tony, tell this man who I am."

Fetterman reached the guard's post and said, "I don't think I know this man."

"Should I shoot him?" asked the guard seriously, as he raised his rifle.

"No, I think I'll take him prisoner instead." Fetterman stepped over the knee-high chain that ran from tree stump to tree stump, marking the border of the tent city. "Morning, sir."

"Morning, Master Sergeant."

"You looking for some coffee or breakfast?"

"Had some coffee already, and I'm not ready for breakfast now. Kepler around?"

"He should be returning at any moment. He took a ride over to MACV for the latest Intelligence. What about our helicopter flying friends?"

"They're beginning to arrive at the choppers already."

Gerber stepped over the chain as a jeep turned onto the street, headed toward them and then stopped. Kepler sat behind the wheel.

"Let's go over to SOG," he said. "Got the latest from G-2 at MACV."

Gerber turned and walked back, stepping over the chain again and climbing into the passenger's side of the jeep.

Fetterman hesitated and then joined them. He spoke to the guard. "Don't shoot anyone. Keep them outside the perimeter until I return, unless you personally recognize them."

"Yes, Master sergeant."

Fetterman hopped up on the rear of the jeep. "Let's go."

Kepler popped the clutch, trying to throw Fetterman into the road, but the master sergeant was hanging on tightly. Kepler spun the wheel, raced along the side of the SOG building and then slammed on the brakes.

As Kepler shut off the engine and locked the wheel, Gerber and Fetterman got out and walked around to the front of the building. Gerber noticed that more of the helicopter crews had arrived. The machine guns were all mounted and there were men crawling over the tops of the choppers.

"So far so good," said Gerber.

When Kepler joined them, they walked into the building and down the hall to the briefing room. Gerber turned on the lights again and Kepler looked to the left.

"Coffee?"

"Go ahead," said Gerber.

"Some for me too," said Fetterman.

Kepler returned a minute later and set the coffee in front of Fetterman. He then sat down and pulled a map out of his pocket. As he spread it out he grinned. "There's a second lieutenant over at MACV that's madder than hell. Screamed and hollered about me writing classified information on my map and not stamping the top and bottom 'secret.' Told me regulations and rules and instructions. Didn't want me to leave with all this good poop written down."

Gerber glanced at the map and understood the significance of the information immediately. He pointed at it. "If we had a straight line, we could anticipate their next target easily and be there waiting. But this is an arc, which means they're probably operating out of a base headquarters in the Boi Loi Woods."

Kepler nodded. "Put the dates of the attacks in and it's even more obvious." He touched the mark farthest to the south. "This is the first indication of something unusual happening. Next here, a little farther to the west, then here and finally here, at Can Me To."

"So," said Fetterman. "We can either wait for them in the vicinity of Mon Hoa here, Trang Hoa here, or actively search for them here, near Bien Tuy."

"My guess would be to search around Bien Tuy," said Gerber. "Everywhere they've hit is within a day's march of their base. That's the place to start."

"We got enough men to hit it?" asked Kepler.

Gerber spun the map and looked at it. "We can pull arty support from Dau Tieng or any of the fire bases in the general area. We could have half our force standing by there if we want.

Move the whole unit before starting the search, though that kind of defeats the purpose of having two complete teams.''

"Hell, Captain, the one in the field can rest at the fire base."

"I suppose so."

"So," said Kepler, "how'd I do?"

"If the information proves out, ya done good."

NEWHAWSER WOKE WITH a pounding headache and the feeling that he was going to throw up at any moment. The bed and the room were spinning, and he knew he should have eaten dinner rather than drinking it.

And then he realized that the pounding wasn't just in his head but at the door. Groaning, he rolled over and pushed his head under the pillow, but that didn't work, and his stomach revolted at the motion.

Finally he forced himself up and stumbled toward the door, opening it and then retreating into the darkness of his room. He sat on the edge of the bed as his stomach churned and his head throbbed.

Rice stood there. "You should have found a lady friend instead of a bottle."

"Long-term effects," said Newhawser. "Your dick might rot off."

"And your liver might be pickled. At least there are drugs to help me save my dick, if that's necessary, but once you've fucked your liver, you've fucked your liver."

"You wouldn't have a Coke, would you?" asked Newhawser quickly.

Rice reached into the pocket of his jungle fatigues and produced a can. "How's that?"

"Beautiful." Newhawser opened it and took a deep drink. That made his head spin faster and the room seemed to pulsate, but he kept on drinking. He stood up suddenly, took another huge swallow and announced, "I think that did it. Excuse me."

He fled the room, pushed his way into the latrine and dropped to the concrete floor in front of a toilet. His stomach convulsed once and nothing happened, but then he threw up again and again.

Finally feeling weak, his body soaked in sweat, he realized that he was finished. He made his way to a sink and washed his face and then washed out his mouth.

Back in his room, Rice had turned on the light and was sitting on the bed flipping through a magazine he'd found lying around. "You feeling better?"

"Much." He put on his fatigues and then plucked a bottle of mouthwash off the dresser. He drank from it, sloshed it around and then swallowed it. "Christ, that's awful."

"Ready?" asked Rice standing up.

"Ready." He grabbed his baseball cap and put it on. He then looked at Rice and asked, "How was she?"

"Hardworking. Tried to convince me that I was absolutely the best thing that had ever happened to her. I was a world champion and all others paled when compared to me. She couldn't live without me."

"And you believed her, right?"

"Hell, I told her if I was that good she could move in with me and I wouldn't even charge her rent. She allowed as how I wasn't all that good and suggested that I move on, alone, preferably in the next minute or so." He tossed the magazine to the side.

"Oh well," said Newhawser.

"So, you up for some breakfast?"

"I think not."

They walked down the hall and out the front door. There was a truck sitting there, the engine running and a couple of other soldiers seated quietly in the back, waiting. "Must be our ride," said Rice.

Hoskinson leaned over the tailgate. "Hey, he's alive. I was sure he'd be dead of alcohol poisoning."

"I'm too short to die in such a ridiculous way," said Newhawser. He climbed in and sat down. "Tell the driver to move slowly."

The last of the ACs joined them, climbing up without a word. Cruz slapped the top of the cab once. "Let's motor, James."

They drove off toward the SOG building as the sun began to come up. They could see the crews climbing over the helicopters.

The truck stopped and the pilots jumped out. Newhawser walked over to his aircraft, looked up at Stockton who was inspecting the rotor head.

"How's it look?"

"We're ready for takeoff whenever you are." He crouched at the rear of the helicopter and slid down quickly to the ground.

Newhawser pushed the cargo compartment door the rest of the way open and pulled out the chicken plates that had been stored under the troop seat. He found his pistol belt, an old-west-style holster complete with loops in the back for extra ammo, and strapped it on low like a gunslinger.

"Let's go to war," said Newhawser.

FETTERMAN AND KEPLER left the briefing room to get the strikers ready to move. Gerber walked out to the helicopters and found Fallon at the rear, twisting the tail rotor as he checked it.

"Got a minute?" asked Gerber.

Fallon let go of the rotor. "Sure."

"We're going to stage out of fire-support base Crazy Horse. Both lifts. One on the choppers and one standing by there."

"No scout ship?" asked Fallon.

"No, we'll still use that, but I want everyone close at hand in case we luck into something quickly."

Fallon moved to the cargo compartment and took his map from the case at the rear of the console. He spread it out and then used a flashlight to look at it. "Show me."

Gerber pointed out the small towns, the location of the fire base and the area they wanted to search.

"Okay. I say we put in the first lift, fly back to Cu Chi for refueling, then head on out, in search mode."

"Fine," said Gerber. "Are you about ready?"

"Give us thirty minutes to complete the preflights and get the aircraft wound up."

Gerber thanked him and walked back to the tent city. Fetterman had the men broken into two main groups, which were further divided into five loads for the helicopters.

"Who's staying behind to watch the tent city?"

"No one," said Fetterman. "Got a couple of men from here to watch it for us while we're out."

"You ready?"

"Whenever we get the sign. We're taking only what we need for the day. I figured we'd either be out by then or we could get resupply by chopper."

Gerber suddenly felt useless. Fallon and the helicopter crews had their duties well in hand, and Fetterman and Kepler had the strikers ready. They'd anticipated his orders and had prepared accordingly.

"Maybe I should just head on back to the hotel and let you handle this."

"If you'd like," said Fetterman.

"Great. Tell me I'm the fifth wheel."

"Yes, sir."

Gerber grinned and then turned, walking back to the SOG building. He entered it and moved to the dayroom where he turned on the radio in time to hear, "GOOOOOOOD MOOORNing, Vietnam. This is Army PFC Pat Sajak."

Gerber wasn't sure if he wanted to listen to Sajak play rock and roll music that early in the morning. Or ever for that matter. But he left the radio on as he stepped to the window and looked at the men crawling over the helicopters, getting them ready for the mission.

Fetterman brought over the first lift, keeping the strikers off to the side, well away from the helicopters. Now Gerber turned off the radio and walked out. The crew chief stood outside of the lead chopper, the cargo door pushed forward so that he could look up on the engine deck as the pilot started the turbine.

The noise level on the tarmac increased as each of the other four helicopters was started. Gerber waited as the wind created by the rotors swept the dust and debris from the ramp, blowing it away.

Then one of the men began waving, and Fetterman understood completely. He led the first of the strikers to the lead helicopter. They climbed in, those on the troop seat buckling their seat belts while the others sat on the floor, hanging on to anything they could find.

Gerber ran across the tarmac, holding down his boonie cap. He carried his M-16 in his left hand. He wore a pistol belt with three canteens, a first aid pack and an ammo pouch holding spare magazines for the pistol he also carried. He climbed into the lead helicopter.

Glancing to the rear, he saw that Fetterman had gotten the rest of the strikers into the choppers. Kepler had boarded the trail ship, but Fetterman had run back across the road. He'd be coming in with the second lift.

The AC turned and looked at him. Gerber raised a thumb, telling him that they were ready. The man nodded and turned his attention to the instruments in front of him.

Rice put his hand on the cyclic and pressed the button for the radio. He called the tower and requested takeoff instructions, explaining that he was a flight of five helicopters at the

SOG pad. He received the wind information and the altimeter setting and was told to wait one. Finally he was told to take off to the south, crossing the runways and then breaking to the west staying low, under the fixed-wing traffic on long final.

Rice lifted up, turned to look at the other aircraft and then keyed the mike, "Lead's on the go."

He turned using the pedals, dropped the nose and made a run across the concrete runways of Tan Son Nhut.

"You're off with five," came the word from the trail aircraft.

"Roger, five."

They raced along the ground, no more than ten feet high, crossed the perimeter where there were bunkers manned by American infantry, and then out into the rice paddies west of Saigon and south of the airfield. They stayed low-level, passed a village of thatch-and-mud hootches where the cooking fires were burning bright, putting out smudges of blue smoke. The people tried hard not to see the helicopters, keeping their heads down as if nothing were happening around them.

Close to Highway One they began a rapid climb to fifteen hundred feet.

"You're joined with five," the trail pilot spoke again.

"Roger. Come up a staggered trail."

A few moments later came the report, "You're formed in staggered trail."

"Roger. Rolling it over."

Fallon took the map out and sat there holding it. He marked off the checkpoints, making sure they were heading in the right direction and that they were on course. He saw the base camp at Cu Chi, the small town of Trang Bang called Gang Bang by everyone in the flight, and Trung Lap. As they passed it, just to the south, they were nearing Hobo Woods. Another twenty klicks and they would be at fire-support base Crazy Horse.

When they were five minutes out, Rice told Fallon to contact the camp and let them know they were inbound. Appar-

ently someone had coordinated the effort because there were
no questions. The RTO said that smoke would be thrown and
they should touch down there.

As they came in, Rice saw a figure spring through the wire,
out onto the open killing field that surrounded the small, circular camp. The man threw a smoke grenade. There was a
flash and it began to billow clouds of purple.

"ID purple," said Rice unnecessarily.

"Roger, purple," the FSB's RTO replied.

The lone man ran back toward the camp. Rice shot the approach to put the nose right over the purple smoke grenade.
He eased off his descent, hovered forward and then landed.

"You're down with five."

The strikers, including Gerber, got out of the cargo compartments, taking their time. No one was in a hurry in the cold
LZ that close to a fire-support base.

When the strikers were out, Trail radioed. "You're unloaded."

"Roger," said Rice. "Let's go get the next load. Lead's on
the go."

As they reached the tree line three hundred yards from the
bunkers of fire-support base Crazy Horse, Trail said, "You're
off with five. Negative fire reported."

12

FIRE-SUPPORT BASE
CRAZY HORSE

When the second lift came in, Gerber ran out to the lead helicopter. Fetterman was sitting on the cargo compartment floor, his back to the armored seat of the peter pilot. He grinned broadly.

"We're ready," said Fetterman. He touched the PRC-25 sitting next to him. "You got a radio?"

"Set and ready." He looked at the master sergeant. "Don't do anything foolish."

"We're just going to look around. Search the ground for signs of the enemy."

"We'll stand by here," said Gerber.

Fetterman nodded and then slipped to the rear, sitting on the edge of the troop seat. He pulled the radio with him, holding it between his feet. "I see anything, I'll pull back and give you a shout."

Gerber held up a thumb and stepped back.

As he retreated, the lead aircraft came to a three-foot hover, hung there motionless momentarily, a cloud of dust wrapping it, and then lifted. In seconds it was gone, the noise with it. The other aircraft had shut down and there was an ominous silence.

Gerber walked down the line until he found Kepler sitting in the rear of the trail chopper. He had a PRC-25 sitting at his feet, the volume turned down so that it only emitted an occasional squeal. There was a small speaker hooked to it so that Kepler didn't have to keep the handset against his head. The speaker could be removed easily, once they moved into the field.

"Now we wait," said Kepler.

Gerber nodded. "Of course."

"And if this doesn't work?"

"Hell, you're the Intel NCO, you tell me. What's our fall back position?"

Kepler leaned back against the gray soundproofing on the transmission wall. He clutched his M-16 in his left hand, the butt sitting on the floor and the barrel pointed toward the top of the chopper. "I can contact my agents and see if they know anything."

Gerber sat down on the edge of the cargo compartment deck and stared at the strands of wire that protected the fire-support base but didn't say anything more. Waiting was always the hardest part.

FETTERMAN WATCHED THE GROUND slip away under him. He sat on the very edge of the troop seat, a map held against his thigh as they flew along, searching for the enemy. The greens were not as bright as they were just after a rain or in the central highlands. There was a dusty look to the land, as if the red dust had been blown up and swirled around by hurricane force winds. Everything had a muddy, reddish-brown and dying look to it. That seemed appropriate.

The trees of the forest were not as thick as they were in the jungle. Fetterman could see to the ground where the grasses and the vines had been worn away, creating paths followed by man and animal. Trails running through the woods gave clues about the settlement patterns in the area.

They flew straight west and then broke to the north, returning about half a klick away from their original flight path. Fetterman, along with the crew chief and the door gunner, searched the ground.

As they flew over a farmer's hootch, Fetterman saw the family bunker with the top wide open. There was no one inside, but some of the earth near it looked as if it had recently been overturned.

There were signs of artillery strikes. Trees stripped of leaves, the trunks graying. There were craters in the ground and splashes of mud.

But there was no sign of enemy activity. No fresh trails through the jungle. No signs of firefights. It was empty land where everyone was afraid to go. The farmers because they might be mistaken for VC or NVA, the enemy because they might be spotted by the Americans. And the Americans, afraid of stirring up a hornets' nest.

Fetterman looked down on all that, his senses attuned to the slightest sign that someone had been down there walking recently. He spotted a trail but it led into a rice paddy where a farmer worked alone. A group of people came into view, but none of them had weapons, and they carried nothing that could easily conceal weapons. More farmers on their way to the fields.

But then, when it looked as if the first round would prove to be fruitless, Fetterman saw two men dive for cover. Just a flash of motion. He wanted a chance for a better look, but knew that if they turned, it would warn the men below that they had been seen. This was the sort of thing that the mission had been designed to exploit.

Over the intercom, Fetterman asked, "Anyone see any movement down there?"

"Thought I saw something," said the door gunner, confirming Fetterman's suspicions.

"You want to return?" asked Fallon.

"No! We keep on going to the east but begin a climb."

"Okay," said Rice.

Fetterman pulled off the headset he'd been wearing and turned on the PRC-25. "Zulu Six, this is Zulu Five."

"This is Six. Go."

"Roger. We've got some movement down here. You want to get your people in motion?"

"Roger. Say location."

Fetterman gave him a set of coordinates they had designed earlier. Gerber rogered him. "We'll be there in one zero minutes."

"Better hurry."

GERBER LEAPED FROM the rear of the helicopter and yelled, "Let's fire them up."

The strikers, who had been playing cards, talking, singing or sleeping, sprang into action. They leaped into the rear of the helicopters. Others from the second force ran back toward the wire of the fire-support base.

The door gunners untied the rotor blades, swung them out, and the air was filled with the sound of the turbines starting. Gerber ran toward the lead aircraft and leaped into the rear. He stuck his face between the seats and yelled, "I've the grid coordinates."

The AC turned and pushed a map at him. "Where?"

Gerber's finger stabbed out. "Here."

"LZ hot or cold?"

"Cold right now but there are armed soldiers in the vicinity."

"Roger." The pilot turned back to his duties.

Gerber slipped to the rear and sat down on the troop seat. In moments the helicopter came up to a three-foot hover. It turned, and seeing that all the other choppers were ready, turned back. They took off, climbing over the trees and heading to the west.

Gerber had a dozen unanswered questions. Fetterman had told them to come, and they were on the way. There hadn't been time to find out exactly what he'd seen. Too much information given over the radio might provide the enemy with hard Intelligence. It might give him the chance to escape. Gerber knew that Fetterman would not scramble them for nothing. He'd have his answers in a few minutes.

The door gunner slapped Gerber on the shoulder and pointed to a single ship out to the north. It moved toward them, caught them and the flight joined on it.

Gerber looked at the strikers in the chopper with him. He yelled at them. "Let's get ready. Everyone out and hit the ground until the choppers are gone."

One man nodded and shouted at the others using their language. One by one they all nodded.

Through the windshield Gerber could see an open field, but it was surrounded by trees. Not the best of landing zones, but they had to touch down somewhere.

As they came in the door guns opened fire. Red tracers flashed, hit the ground in front of the trees and some of them bounced, tumbling. At first, there were only M-60s firing. A hammering that could be heard over the sound of the helicopter engines and rotors.

Then closer to the ground, more firing erupted. This was hidden in the trees. Flashes from the muzzles of automatic weapons. Green tracers coming up at them. One slammed into the windshield, punching through it. A tiny network of cracks appeared. But the helicopter didn't waver. It stuck in the flight.

Gerber slipped from the troop seat and crouched in the door. He studied the trees as they came up to greet him. Muzzle-flashes strobing. Red tracers lancing downward.

And then they were on the ground. Gerber leaped, ran and dived to the dirt. Around him there was more firing. Strikers squeezing the triggers of their weapons. Dirt fountained. There was smoke in the air. Noise from the helicopters and the firing. A grenade. Shrapnel whirling.

Gerber spotted an enemy and fired at him. Nothing. Others were on the ground around him, shooting.

The helicopters lifted as one. The door guns had fallen silent as the choppers landed, but began to shoot again. They raked the trees, shredding them. Bark, bits of wood and leaves rained down.

RICE HAD KNOWN it was going to be a hot LZ. They had seen the enemy soldiers earlier and they were now going after them. There would be shooting. He just hoped it was one or two NVA with AKs. The door guns could suppress those easily and quickly. If there was much more they could get chopped up, especially since there was no gun support available.

As they turned inbound, he touched the intercom. "Wallace, you warn these guys to get out fast. We land and they're gone immediately."

"Yes, sir."

To Fallon he said, "You get on the controls with me and follow my movements."

"Okay."

"If I'm hit, the closest evac facility is at Dau Tieng. For major wounds, you might be better just rolling it over for Cu Chi. You know the freq for the evac hospitals?"

"Six two decimal five."

"Inbound you tell them what you have. Describe the wounds to them so they can prepare."

"Understood."

Over the radio he said, "Full suppression."

"You're up trail," said the pilot in the trail aircraft.

"Roger, Trail."

Rice descended so that they were now just over the tops of the trees, the skids no more than five or ten feet from them. He had rolled over so that they were flying along at nearly a hundred knots.

"We're about a klick out," said Rice.

In front of them was the clearing. An open area in the tops of the trees. He aimed at it, figuring on slowing as he approached. The problem was the four aircraft behind him. He had to plan for them, too. They wouldn't be able to follow violent movements. It became hard to lead when it seemed the entire North Vietnamese Army was shooting at you, and one guy with an AK could seem like the whole North Vietnamese Army. The temptation was to roll over and get the hell out.

"Coming up on the LZ," said Rice. "Slowing it down." He pulled back on the cyclic and dropped the collective so they didn't gain any altitude.

Half a klick from the clearing he began a slight climb to bleed off the airspeed and give him a better angle for the landing. Without the flight he would have pulled a gravity stop, but that was much too violent a maneuver for the flight to follow.

Suddenly the door guns opened fire. A hammering behind him. Out of the corner of his eyes he saw the ruby-colored tracers flashing into the tree line.

"Flight's taking fire on the left," said Newhawser over the radio.

Rice heard the single AK and ignored it. Over the intercom Wallace shouted, "I see him! I see him." And at the same moment he started pouring a stream of fire into the trees where the enemy soldier hid.

More firing erupted. The tree line sparkled in the late-morning sun. Flashes of light from the muzzles of the enemy weapons. First just the one, then two and finally half a dozen. Rice could hear them firing over the sound of the turbine and the pounding of his own weapons.

As they crossed the edge of the tree line and Rice pulled back to slow them, a shot snapped through the windshield. The sharp crack splattered Plexiglas over him. A flying shard cut his jaw.

Then suddenly they were down in the LZ and the door guns stopped firing. He heard Wallace shouting, "Go! Go! Go!"

"Down with five. Fire on the left."

"Lead's on the go."

"Taking fire on the left."

Rice sucked in the pitch and dumped the nose. The door guns began to shoot again. More firing from the trees. And some from the men on the ground. M-16s and AKs and M-60s. There was an explosion. Maybe a grenade.

"You're off with five." Over the radio he could hear the sound of the door guns from trail.

Suddenly they were over the edge of the tree line again and the firing from the door guns stopped. From far behind he could hear the battle on the ground, surprised that it could cut through the roaring turbine and the popping rotor blades.

"You're out with five."

Rice relaxed slightly. He continued the climb, slowing to sixty knots so that the other aircraft would have a chance to catch up.

"Anyone take any hits?"

"Trail took a few in the tail boom."

"Roger."

"Lead, you're joined with five."

"Roger. Lead's rolling it over. Let's stay in a straight trail formation."

He turned slowly to the east, heading back to fire-support base Crazy Horse, cruising at fifteen hundred feet. As AFVN played rock and roll over the ADF, he realized what a crazy war it was. Kids flying in and out of combat, listening to the same music that their counterparts in the World listened to as they drove to and from the Saturday football games.

WHEN THE CHOPPERS were gone, Fetterman was up and running toward the trees. Gerber knew that their only hope for survival was to get out of the open. He joined Fetterman, running at the enemy force, firing from the hip.

He screamed at the strikers. "Let's go! Let's go! Hit the trees."

One man got up, took a bullet in the chest and fell backward. Blood spurted from his wound, the jet almost three feet high. The second was smaller and the third a bubbling froth. The man had bled to death quickly.

But they couldn't stop for him. The men were all running toward the trees. Some were screaming. They were firing their weapons. One man stopped and threw a grenade. It detonated in the trees, throwing up a cloud of red dust and black smoke. More firing came from the enemy. A machine gun opened up and then stopped suddenly.

Gerber sprinted forward. He saw Fetterman dive into the trees and heard a wild burst of firing there. Then he was in the trees too. He leaped over a fallen log and saw two enemy soldiers. He kicked at one and spun, firing at the other. As that man collapsed, Gerber whirled and shot again. The bullet struck the man on the side of the nose, blowing out the back of his head. He flopped down, kicked his feet as if trying to push himself backward, and then died.

There was firing all around him. M-16s and AK-47s. Some on full-auto. Men were screaming, some in rage and others in pain. An NVA soldier appeared and fired one shot. Gerber heard it snap by his head. He fired from the hip. His round took the enemy in the stomach, throwing him back. He disappeared into the thick vegetation.

As the man died, Gerber pushed forward. He saw two men running. Dropping to one knee, he fired once, twice, three times. One of the soldiers was hit. He slammed into a tree face first and then slipped to the ground. The other got away.

Suddenly around him the firing was tapering. Now he could only hear the M-16s, some of them on full-auto. M-79s were blooping out grenades. There were quiet explosions deep in the trees. Dust and smoke swirled up in the distance.

"That's it," yelled Gerber. "Everyone hold. Everyone hold. Cease fire."

He turned and ran along the line. There was a striker lying facedown on the ground, blood pooling under him. Gerber dropped to one knee, reaching for the throat to get the pulse and then saw the exit wound in the man's side. A huge hole that exposed bone and internal organs. Swarming black flies had already began to collect on the wound. Their buzzing was easily audible, even over the fading sounds of the battle.

He got up and ran on. He spotted Fetterman kneeling next to a tree, his weapon aimed into the forest. He was watching as the strikers moved through the trees, clearing the last of the NVA and collecting the dropped weapons.

"What you got?"

"NVA, sir. Took off. A rear guard at best."

"Did their job," said Gerber. "We'll have to hold here to evac the wounded."

"I could take a squad forward for a recon."

"Let's get the situation stabilized here first." He reached up and wiped the sweat from his face. He realized that the firing was now sporadic. Single shots from M-16s.

Kepler appeared, dragging a dead man with him. He was dressed as a VC but it was obvious from his haircut he was NVA. Kepler dropped him to the ground and said, "Thought you'd want to see one of the enemy up close."

"He tell you anything?"

"He's NVA and not VC," said Kepler. "You can see he's dressed as VC. Got a new AK with Russian writing on it, not a Chicom copy. He carried no personal papers or wallet. Well trained, though not their best."

"Told you a lot for a dead man," said Gerber, looking down at the body.

"You just have to know what to look for." Kepler crouched next to the corpse.

"Okay, Derek. Thanks." He turned toward Fetterman. "Let's get this situation stabilized then," he said. "I need a head count, and someone had better check the wounded. Our wounded. We need to get them evaced."

"Yes, sir."

"HORNET LEAD, this is Zulu Six."

Fallon touched the floor button and said, "Go, Six."

Rice said, "You're still on the intercom."

Fallon nodded and turned the selector to the number-one position and said again, "Go, Six."

"We need Medevac and we need the second lift," said Gerber over the radio.

"Roger."

Rice shot a glance at Fallon and then made his own call. "Ah, Six, understand you want us to bring in the second lift and evac the wounded at that time."

"That's a roger."

In the distance he saw the circular pattern of the fire-support base. He turned toward it then and began the gradual letdown for landing. As they neared, someone threw a smoke grenade that produced a cloud of green. Watching it, Rice realized that they were coming in downwind. He eased off the approach, circled around to the north and then came in again, this time into the wind.

They touched down and almost the instant the skids hit the ground, the strikers swarmed toward them, climbing into the cargo compartments. They sat on the troop seat, on the floor and against the armored seats. A couple sat in the doors, their feet hanging out.

"Lead, you're down with five and loaded."

"Roger."

And the process could start all over again.

13

THE BOI LOI WOODS
WEST OF FIRE-SUPPORT
BASE CRAZY HORSE

While Gerber and the others retreated to the LZ so that they could get the dead and wounded evaced, Fetterman and a squad of twelve began to push forward, following the fleeing enemy soldiers. He'd selected good NCOs and a single officer to go with him. Men whose training was a little better than the privates and corporals. Men who had performed well in the short, violent firefight.

Now they were moving quietly through the thin forest, using the shadows and the cover as they followed the NVA. Fetterman was out front, walking slowly, his head swiveling right and left, studying everything around him. He was worried because the NVA didn't seem to be concerned about covering the line of their retreat. That might mean they were all frightened, running away as fast as they could, or it might mean they didn't care because they were leading Fetterman and his tiny force into a death trap.

Fetterman suspected that they had run into a rear guard composed of the second-line troops. Men who weren't as well trained as the others. That explained the rapid breakdown in the fight and the obvious trail they were leaving as they tried to escape. That was what he expected, but he was prepared for the worst.

He stopped periodically, listening. The men fanned out slightly, forming a circle so they could protect one another from a sudden attack. Fetterman crouched in the shade of a dying palm tree. Sweat soaked his jungle fatigues, and he wanted a drink of water but didn't take it.

He studied the ground in front of him. There wasn't much grass cover. Knee-high bushes and trees fifteen or twenty feet tall, the branches twisted around as if they had been subjected to a constant pressure to mutate them. Some of the branches were bare, the leaves stripped by firefights, air strikes and artillery. The trunks of some were light gray, killed by shrapnel that stripped the bark, leaving the trunks bare and exposed to the sun. The ground vegetation seemed to grow up to the trunks so that it looked as if the trees were growing out of a green lake. The sun beat down, baking the ground around them. It was hot and humid, but not as bad as it sometimes got in the thickest jungle. A light breeze blew through here.

When Fetterman was sure that no one waited in ambush and that no one was following him, he waved a hand and started forward again. The broken bushes and the stirred-up dirt pointed him in the right direction. He spotted a piece of equipment, a chest pouch for AK magazines. He pointed it out to the others and shook his head telling them to leave it. A booby-trapped souvenir would stop them.

But the men with him were well disciplined. Each of them might have been tempted, but each of them resisted that temptation. They passed the pouch, leaving it right where the NVA soldier had thrown it.

Again, fifteen minutes later, Fetterman stopped. The trees were getting thicker now. The breeze was rattling the leaves, masking the sound that his squad was making, but also hiding the sound the enemy might make. Now there was a dimness in the forest, created by the canopy. Patches of light and dark and gray. Men could hide in that pattern easily, but Fetterman saw nothing of them.

They started forward slowly, the pace nowhere as fast as it had been. There was too much cover, too many opportunities to make mistakes. Besides, the enemy was blazing a trail for them.

They moved for another ten minutes and the trail suddenly fanned out, almost like a narrow stream that washed onto an alluvial plain. Everyone went in a different direction all at once. That could only mean one thing.

Fetterman halted them and then forced a retreat of fifty yards. He found the RTO, took the handset from him and whispered into it, "Zulu Six, Zulu Six, this is Zulu Five, over."

"This is Six. Go."

"Roger, Six, I believe we have located the enemy's base, over."

"Understood. We will follow you in one zero minutes, over."

"Roger that. We will stand by here. Out."

GERBER CROUCHED at the edge of the tree line, looking out into the LZ where the two covered bodies of the strikers lay. Near them were seven wounded men. Two of them weren't hurt badly and could have stayed, except that the medic had wanted to get them out. He was afraid of infection, which quickly became deadly in the tropical environment.

The radio came alive again. "Zulu Six, this is Hornet Lead. Can you throw smoke?"

"Roger, smoke." Gerber took a smoke grenade, pulled the pin and then threw it into the center of the LZ.

"ID red."

"Roger, red."

"Understand LZ is now cold."

"LZ is cold. Will you be taking out the wounded now?" asked Gerber.

"Roger, that."

Gerber then heard the sound of the helicopters. He looked and saw them in the distance, just over the tops of the trees, looking like huge insects.

Gerber stood up, holding his M-16 in his left hand. Behind him, scattered in a semicircle about fifty yards in the trees were the strikers. They were insuring that the NVA didn't filter back in to take a few shots at the choppers in the hopes of bringing one down.

The helicopters came in slowly and landed in swirling clouds of dust and dry grass. The strikers leaped from the rear as the wounded climbed on the trail chopper, taking the two dead men with them.

Kepler loped across the LZ and along the trees until he found Gerber. "They made it."

"Let's get the men organized and ready to go. I think Tony's located their base."

"Yes, sir. Two minutes at the most."

The helicopters were off then, flying over the tops of the trees. Gerber took the handset and squeezed it. "Hornet Lead, why don't you refuel now and then stand by at the fire base."

"Roger, that. We'll be out of touch for about thirty minutes."

Gerber didn't like the sound of that, but once they had gotten refueled and standing by, they'd be in a better position to assist if necessary. There would be no worries about suddenly running out of fuel.

"Hornet Lead, can you leave us one ship?"

"Will have Hornet Three standing by over the LZ. Be advised that we'll break trail off to take the wounded to the hospital."

"I understand your problem."

"Roger, that."

Gerber gave the handset back to the RTO. "Let's get the men moving, Derek. Compass course of two nine one. You take the point now and I'll bring up the rear."

"Yes, sir."

Kepler disappeared into the trees. Gerber rounded up the rest of the strikers, getting them moving. He kept three with him and they moved into the forest. Kepler was ready, and as Gerber appeared, he stepped out. The column strung out so that each man was five or six yards from the man in front of him. They didn't expect trouble, not with Fetterman sitting on the path at the far end, but the NVA were sometimes tricky, doubling back to attack when it was least expected.

Kepler kept the pace steady. He stopped once for a quick break, letting the strikers drink some of their water. The biggest problem they faced in the field other than enemy soldiers was dehydration in the late-morning heat.

They moved west, easing through the forest. After thirty minutes they halted again. Gerber walked along the line and caught up with Kepler, who was now talking to Fetterman.

When Gerber approached he whispered, "What you got here?"

Fetterman turned and looked to the west. "We've got some kind of bunker-and-tunnel complex. You can see the tops of some of the bunkers, and we've found one spider hole and one trapdoor down into a shallow tunnel."

"Any sign of the enemy?"

Fetterman shook his head. "We circled the outside of the camp carefully but there's no sign that the enemy left it anytime in the past five, six hours. I think there are some NVA hiding in there."

"Derek?"

"Seems that the rear guard is now holed up here. More important, there might be some things of Intelligence value inside. We might learn what's happening with the assassination squad."

"Tony?"

"Sweep in and clear it one bunker at a time. Grenades and rifles to do it, but keep the majority of the men under cover until we either capture the place or need to attack it in force."

"Derek," said Gerber, "take a squad out to the south and then set up a blocking force there in case they break out in that direction. I want you to be able to watch the western and southern sides."

"Yes, sir."

"Tony, I'll do the same on the north, and then you move in carefully. You get into trouble and we'll all assault toward the center."

"Ten minutes?"

"Right. Let's do it." Gerber moved off and found one of the NCOs. He pointed to fifteen men and motioned for them to follow him. Kepler did the same thing.

Gerber walked to the north and then to the west. Through gaps in the trees and bushes, he could see the center area where the bunker complex lay. When he had gotten far enough to the west, he halted his people and positioned them. The majority were facing the bunkers. There were two men on each side facing either east or west so they couldn't be flanked. Two men were posted to the rear to watch for an enemy surprise attack from that direction.

He checked his watch, peeling the camouflage cover from it. Seven minutes had passed. Fetterman would be moving into the bunker complex soon.

FETTERMAN WATCHED the last few seconds tick off, then waved his men forward. They worked their way toward the bunker line, leapfrogging past one another. They reached the end of the line and halted. Fetterman lay on the dead leaves in a patch of shade and studied the bunkerline. He could see a couple of the firing ports and into the rear of one. He tried to spot movement, but it seemed that all the bunkers close to him were empty.

Satisfied, he got up and ran forward, staying away from the firing port of the first bunker. He leaped, landing at the side of it. Around him, the strikers infiltrated, penetrating the line in three other positions. They moved quickly and silently.

Fetterman crawled forward and glanced to the rear of the bunker. With the sun and the trees where they were, it was impossible to see the interior. Fetterman pulled a grenade, yanked the pin free and tossed the grenade into the rear of the bunker. He scrambled back and lay flat. The grenade detonated with a dull, flat bang, and Fetterman was up, diving into the boiling smoke in the rear of the bunker.

Inside there was nothing to see. It smelled of old dirt. Light filtered in through the firing port, creating a bright shaft and a square on the floor. Fetterman probed the corners with his weapon, but they were solid. No one was hiding there, and there were no trapdoors or tunnel entrances.

Around him there were a couple of other explosions. Dull pops as more grenades went off. The strikers were clearing bunkers too.

Fetterman moved to the rear and crouched there. He heard a single shot. At the sound he leaped out and rolled, turning toward the direction of the discharge. He recognized it as an AK-47.

Suddenly there were men running all over the bunker complex. Fetterman opened fire. A short bust took a running NVA soldier in the back. He was lifted from his feet and thrown down. He rolled over and was still.

Firing erupted all around them. AKs and M-16s. Fetterman saw one of his men fall. Two enemy soldiers ran at the body. Fetterman fired at them. The first was hit. He spun and fell. The second dived for cover, but Fetterman shot him in the head as he peeked up.

"Fall back," ordered Fetterman.

He stood and fired from the hip. He backed up and then stopped. There were muzzle-flashes from one of the bunkers. Someone firing out the door. An RPD opened up, the rounds snapping through the air. Fetterman saw a steady stream of green tracers.

He dived for cover. He jerked another grenade and pulled the pin. He waited, searching for a target and then spotted the machine gun. He leaped up, threw it and dropped down again.

The grenade detonated. Dirt and debris were thrown up and rained down. But the RPD stopped firing. There were several screams.

Then from the north came more shooting. M-16s and M-79s. The grenades from them exploding in sequence. There was shouting and screaming and whistles.

Fetterman crawled forward and surveyed the situation. "To the right," he shouted. "Pin them down on the right."

Two weapons opened fire. An AK responded. The bullets hit the top of the bunker, throwing up dirt that splattered Fetterman. He dropped down, waited and then popped up, squeezing off two shots.

"Hit them," he yelled.

There was a shout from the right and Fetterman whirled. Two NVA soldiers ran at him. Fetterman fired once and one of them collapsed. The other jumped at Fetterman. They collided and fell together. Fetterman lost his rifle. The enemy tried to shoot him, but the bullet missed, burying itself in the ground.

The master sergeant rolled and shoved the barrel to the side. He grabbed the man's head, holding it and then slamming his forehead into the bridge of the enemy's nose. The man screamed and lost his grip on his weapon. Fetterman spun and tossed the man to the ground. Whipping his knife from its scabbard, he plunged the blade into his opponent's chest.

As that soldier died, so did the firing near him. There was some screaming, orders in Vietnamese. One man leaped into the air and fell. It seemed that the enemy was charging into Gerber's blocking force.

GERBER KNEW THAT the first grenades were Fetterman and the strikers clearing the bunkers. But then the shooting started and he knew that they had found the rear guard from the LZ. A few men firing at first and then more and more until it seemed to be one loud, sustained detonation.

He glanced at the man to his right. The striker knelt there, the M-16 held in both his hands. He was squeezing it and twisting it, as if to insure himself that it was real.

"Steady. Steady," said Gerber.

He saw shadows moving in the distance, but wouldn't allow the men to fire. He wanted to be sure of the targets, and he wanted his unit's presence to be an unpleasant surprise.

The firing decreased and there was shouting from the bunker complex. Then suddenly the NVA were running, almost right at them.

"Now!" yelled Gerber. "NOW!"

He opened fire, picking his targets. One of the enemy soldiers fell, rolling. He tried to get up and was hit again, the bullet blowing off the top of his head. The man collapsed and kicked his feet. It looked as if he was going to stand again, but then he was still.

The strikers switched to full-auto, M-16s hammering. Rounds snapped through the air. They struck the trees around them, shaking them. Bits of bark and leaf fell. The odor of cordite, of excrement and copper, seemed to fill the air.

There was shouting in the bunker complex. The enemy surged toward Gerber and the strikers. One of the strikers threw down his M-16 and ran, but the others held fast. They poured out rounds. The enemy stumbled and fell, and those who weren't hit, suddenly turned around, running back toward the bunkers.

"Cease fire!" yelled Gerber. "Cease fire."

The firing around him slowly tapered and then stopped. Suddenly it was quiet around him except for the moaning of the wounded and the dying.

The radio crackled and Gerber picked up the handset. "Zulu Six."

"Five here. We've captured the rest of the enemy. Threw down their weapons and surrendered."

"I don't like it," said Gerber.

"Neither do I," said Fetterman.

"Fall back to the main body," ordered Gerber. "We'll sweep forward from here."

"Roger."

Gerber threw the handset back to the RTO. He stood up and waved his men forward. He stepped toward the closest downed enemy soldier and pulled the AK away from him. The bullet hole in the center of the man's forehead had killed him.

The line moved from the cover of the trees and out onto the bunker complex. First they checked the bodies scattered around them, taking the weapons so that a possum playing NVA with a suicide complex wouldn't kill a couple of them first. Afterward they began to clear the bunkers. They used grenades to make sure that no one hid in them. When the smoke cleared, they entered, searching. They pulled weapons, boxes, rations and rucksacks from the rubble, tossing it all onto the ground.

Kepler's men swept in from the south, clearing that end of the complex. When they reached Gerber's troops near the center, they stopped. Kepler then slipped back, making a circuit of the bunkers, picking up everything that looked to be of interest.

His main concern was not the identity of the unit, but their plans. He searched the rucks looking for information, documents, scraps that might provide him with a clue about the assassination squad.

Gerber stationed the men around the complex to defend it if they had to. Fetterman brought up the rest of the strike team and filled in. Wounded were treated, and the dead wrapped in poncho liners.

"Got a couple of men who need to be evaced, Captain," Fetterman said.

"Immediately?"

"The sooner the better."

Gerber studied the forest around them. Light trees but nowhere for a chopper to set down.

"Clearing with some light scrub about fifty yards to the east," said Fetterman. "We could clear that and bring in a single ship."

"Do it."

"Yes, sir."

Kepler came forward with a rucksack in his hand. Without a word he opened it, showing Gerber the documents inside. He pulled a handful of them out so that Gerber could see exactly what he had.

"That what I think it is?" asked Gerber.

Kepler nodded. "It's the complete operating instructions of the enemy terrorist squad along with a unit history, list of names of the members and their qualifications and an itinerary. Nearly everything we need."

"So where are they?"

Kepler shrugged. "It's going to take me a little while to work through this."

"Thirty minutes," said Gerber.

"Might take longer," said Kepler. "And this might not be all of it. We've got to collect as much of this as we can for the Intelligence value."

"Then destroy the complex," said Fetterman.

"We don't have time to do that properly," said Gerber. "About the only thing we can do is call in an airstrike and then have someone else assess the damage."

"Which is fine," said Fetterman.

"Let's get at it then," said Gerber.

14

THE JUNGLE
NORTHWEST OF CAN ME
TO

Nhu crouched in the shade of a coconut palm, the sweat dripping down his face and the hunger gnawing at his empty belly. A handful of cold rice washed down with a cupful of water in the morning was not enough to keep a man from feeling hungry. It was enough to maintain his strength for a few days in the jungle, but not enough to satisfy him.

Around him were the members of his squad. All of them knew that something had happened in the jungle behind them a few hours earlier. The sounds of firing had drifted on the light breeze toward them, and they knew the Americans had tracked them to the camp. The rear guard had not done its job. When the firing began, they had quickened their pace, rushing forward until the air burned their lungs, until their legs ached and they thought they would have to stop. But they had reached their destination without the Americans catching them. One more mission and then escape into the safety of Cambodia. No more hiding in the jungle, hoping that the Americans didn't follow them or that American planes didn't bomb them.

The hamlet in front of them looked peaceful enough. There were a few people moving in it. An old woman sat behind a black pot, stirring it slowly, her mouth moving rapidly as she chewed betel nut. Two children ran around a hootch, and an ox was tethered to a pole. Smoke from cooking fires drifted on the breeze.

There seemed to be no one and nothing in the village that would be of interest to them, but Van had brought them here. He had stopped them inside the trees and then spread them out so that he could study the scene in front of them.

As they sat there watching, Nhu slowly took out his canteen and drank from it. The water was warm and tasted of metal, but that didn't matter to him. It quenched his thirst.

He put the canteen away and waited as the sun baked the ground and the jungle. Heat seemed to shimmer in the distance, making the village shiver and shimmy. Two men entered, both wearing black shorts and sandals and carrying tools. They disappeared into a hootch and didn't come back out.

More men began to slip from the surrounding rice fields, returning from a day at work. Young women and children came with them. The population of the village grew. Some of the newcomers stopped by the old woman at the pot while others simply ignored her.

Van stood suddenly and waved his men forward. Nhu got to his feet but didn't leave the protection of the jungle until he had scanned the sky above him. There was no sign of American helicopters or jet fighters.

The men moved from the trees, holding their weapons down along their sides as if that would conceal them. The old woman saw them and shouted a warning to the others, her voice high, the words strained.

But the warning had no effect on the village. The people still moved slowly, never looking toward the oncoming soldiers, as if afraid to see them. Like all the farmers in South Vietnam, they'd learned to pay no attention to the men who made war. That only invited their anger and death.

As the NVA squad moved into the village, they fanned out slightly so that they could cover more ground. From one side, near the last hootch on the northern edge of the hamlet, a man sprinted. A young man wearing only black pajama bottoms. He carried nothing in his hands.

Van dropped to one knee and aimed at the fleeing man. The NVA leader tracked the man, the rifle barrel moving with the target. Finally came a single shot. The running man pitched from a rice paddy dike and sprawled in the warm brown water, facedown. He didn't move. A ragged crimson stain, barely visible from the village, spread around him.

The line began to move again, but the villagers didn't react. Either to the approaching soldiers or to the shot. No one ran out to look at the man or to help him. He had earned his fate, whatever it was. No one else was going to do a thing about it.

They reached the village and stopped walking. One soldier looked into a hootch, shouted something and then disappeared inside it. An instant later a naked woman was shoved into the bright sunlight. She was followed by a naked man. It was obvious to all what they had been doing.

Van pointed at them and began to laugh. He then motioned the two people forward. The woman didn't know what to do with her hands, but the man did. He kept them covering his crotch.

The line moved again toward the center of the village, the man and woman propelled ahead of them. Once there, Van and his men formed a rough circle with the naked people in the center.

"The rest of the villagers," said Van. "Get them and bring them here."

Half of his men peeled out of the formation and began to run through the hamlet shouting orders. They ran into hootches and then out again, pushing people along in front of them. There was a shot. Van turned toward the sound, but didn't move because there were no others.

One of the men appeared then, carrying an M-16. He threw it into the dirt near the two naked people.

"You have been harboring the enemy," said Van. "I knew it. You are all the enemies of the revolution. Every one of you is an enemy of the revolution, and I must make an example of all of you."

No one looked at him as he spoke. They all kept their eyes on the ground at their feet.

"Who is the headman here?"

Again there was silence.

"The headman," demanded Van. He stepped toward the center of the ring, where the villagers now stood. "Tell me."

But no one told him. They stood silently, refusing to look at him and refusing to answer.

Van grabbed the shirt of an old man, yanking him forward. He jerked the man's head up so that he could see his victim's eyes. "Is it you, old man?" he asked. "Is it you?"

The old man remained silent, but stared back at Van, almost in defiance.

"Ah, a spark. A man with a backbone," announced Van. "I like that. Maybe you're not afraid of me, old man." Van raised a hand as if to strike, but didn't.

The old man continued to stare.

Van shrugged, twisted around and stuck the barrel of his weapon into the belly of the old man. Before anyone could react, Van pulled the trigger. The bullet punched through the soft tissues and blew out the old man's back, splattering the ground with blood and tissue. The man staggered back a step and then seemed to sit down hard. He looked up at Van and then fell to his back. Blood bubbled from his mouth as he died.

"Who is the headman?" asked Van again. "If you don't tell me, I'll be forced to shoot everyone."

The threat didn't work. No one spoke. They stood staring at their feet.

Now Van grinned. "Your village will cease to exist today. Your families will cease to exist today. Everything about you will cease. All because you chose to defy me and the People's Army of Liberation."

"I am the village elder," said a man finally as he stepped forward.

Van turned to him and studied him. A young man with jet black hair, big brown eyes and a stocky build. "You seem to be very young for one of such responsibility."

"It is the way," said the man. "The old ones are frightened. Frightened of you, of the Americans, of the war and of the night. Leadership requires someone who is not afraid."

"Admirable," said Van. "But fatal." He didn't hesitate. He fired again. The young man fell to his side, moaning. Van walked slowly to him, pressed the barrel of his AK against the man's temple and pulled the trigger. The top of his skull blew off.

"Now," said Van, "who is the headman?"

It didn't surprise him when no one spoke up.

MORROW RETURNED TO the city room and tried to figure out just what in the hell was going on. Press briefings that hinted at VC and NVA atrocities, but that ended abruptly when the questioning got too intense. A young inexperienced officer giving the briefing when it should have been someone with a little better feel for the operation of the press. Someone who knew how to answer reporters' questions.

That all meant one of two things. Either the story was so unimportant they didn't want to waste valuable time on it, or it was very important and they were trying to disguise it. The second possibility seemed more likely.

Morrow felt a sudden quickening of her pulse, just as she did every time she knew that a good story was within reach. The military rarely tried to be devious, feeling that good press relations would allow them to control, at least in a small way, the stories that were printed in the World. It never worked that way, but the military hadn't learned the lesson yet.

Or maybe they had learned it. She pulled open her top drawer to get a pad and a pen. When she did, she saw the letter that Karen had written her about her upcoming marriage. The letter that had thrown Robin into a downward spiral of depression the past two days.

Now she laughed and shoved it out of the way. She didn't have time to worry about the antics of her sister twelve thousand miles away. There was a story to be found and to be written. Karen and her wedding would just have to wait until the story was finished.

Hodges walked over to her desk and parked a haunch on it. He swung his dangling foot and stared down at her. "You learn anything interesting at the briefing?"

Morrow sat up and crossed her legs slowly. She rubbed her chin and said, "There wasn't much in the briefing, but what wasn't there spoke volumes. When they try to downplay an aspect of the war, it makes me suspicious."

"So, what do you have?"

"There's a terrorist squad operating in this area. The mission would be to frighten the locals into supporting the VC and the NVA. Assassinations and beatings."

"This will work?"

Morrow shrugged. "You see the enemy operate with impunity and you see them kill your friends, you're going to work with them."

"The Nazis tried that and found it didn't work."

"And the Soviets have made it work. It all depends on the situation and the extent to which you'll push."

Hodges nodded. "What's your next move?"

"I'm going to talk to Mack and see if he can provide any insight."

"Is he around?"

"Off and on," said Morrow.

"Then why not talk to Jerry Maxwell over at MACV? Maybe he knows something that'll help."

Morrow shrugged. "This doesn't seem like something the CIA would be in on."

"No," said Hodges, standing, "but he might be able to tell you where to go. That sort of covert operation is something that the CIA would be aware of if not participating in."

"All right," said Morrow. "I'll check with him a little later."

"See if you can't have something worked up for the six o'clock feed."

"I can give you the terrorist statistics for the last year," she said, pulling a sheet of paper from a file folder. "Last year, that is, nineteen sixty-seven, more than nine thousand people were killed or abducted, and this year over ten thousand if you figure in the Tet offensive. Hell, I've got a picture taken in nineteen sixty-six of the bodies of South Vietnamese chained together before they were shot by the Vietcong."

"Old news," said Hodges. "No one wants to read about North Vietnamese killing South Vietnamese unless it just happened."

"Then right now I've got nothing except the murder of the school-teacher."

"See what you can dig up on that. People can identify with that. School-teacher murdered for teaching the kids. That might fly."

"Misses the point, doesn't it?" asked Morrow.

"I'm not concerned with points, I'm more concerned with filling our news hole."

Morrow took a deep breath. "I'll see what I can find."

"I'll need it quickly," said Hodges as he retreated toward his glass cubicle.

THEY GOT THEIR DEAD and wounded, along with the NVA prisoners, lifted out from the small LZ. It wasn't that far from the NVA bunker complex. Kepler had coordinated an interrogation with Military Intelligence at Cu Chi. Then, having completed a search of the area, picking up weapons, documents and anything else that might be useful, they retreated half a klick. Gerber, along with an RTO and a squad for security, halted on a high point that allowed him to look back toward the bunker complex. While Fetterman and Kepler worked their way to the LZ near Can Me To, Gerber called in the artillery to destroy the enemy camp.

He watched as the first round roared overhead and exploded in the jungle. He missed the orange-yellow flash of the detonation, but saw the smoke filtering up through the trees.

"Right one hundred. Add one hundred," said Gerber over the radio.

"Shot, over."

"Shot, out."

The process was repeated but this time the blue-white smoke was right on target.

"Fire for effect," said Gerber.

"Rounds on the way."

The first six rounds were high-explosive, set to detonate on the ground and drive the enemy from their holes. The detonations rocked the ground. There was a second six and then a third. The fourth group was antipersonnel, designed to air-burst, spraying shrapnel down onto anyone who had failed to find protection in the target zone. Then the process was repeated.

Finally the voice on the radio said, "Last rounds on the way. Can you assess the damage?"

Gerber was tempted. If the artillery hadn't done the job, he could call them again, but time was slipping away. They could send out a patrol from fire-support base Crazy Horse just as easily, and accomplish the same thing.

"That's a negative," said Gerber.

"Roger. Thanks for the exercise."

"Out," said Gerber. He gave the handset back to the RTO. To the men he said, "Let's get moving."

They climbed down from the high point and slipped into the forest with one of the strikers on the point. He held his compass out in front of him as if it were some kind of talisman that would lead him to his destination. Gerber checked the direction of march periodically to make sure they hadn't slipped from the proper path.

They had to cross one narrow stream. Each of the men splashed water into his face to wash away the sweat of the march and the grime of the battle. Then, refreshed, they hurried toward the LZ.

When they arrived, Fetterman and Kepler already had the men split into loads for the five helicopters. Kepler was with the first load, kneeling down, reading more of the documents that they had recovered.

Gerber took his men over to where Fetterman stood with those who wouldn't be going on the first lift out. When he arrived, he asked, "You have security out?"

"Couple of listening posts in the trees to warn us if the enemy is approaching."

"I didn't see them," said Gerber.

Fetterman grinned. "They saw you."

"How long before the flight is here?"

"When the LP reported you close, I called for the choppers. About five, ten minutes is all."

"Kepler learn anything?"

"Not yet. He's still trying to come up with a location of the assassination squad."

"I'll go over and talk to him."

"Yes, sir."

Gerber walked across the LZ, the grass no more than three or four inches high. It was dusty from the helicopter landings earlier. If he had turned around, he could have followed his path back to where Fetterman stood.

"You got anything, Derek?"

Kepler looked up as Gerber approached. "I don't have a time frame," he said.

"Meaning?"

"Simply that I know where they've been and where they're going. Now, given that they were in Can Me To a couple of days ago, I can figure where they should be. But there's no real evidence of it."

"So what's the problem?"

Kepler stood up, the documents clutched in his left hand, his weapon in his right. "Villages are ten, twelve, fifteen klicks apart. Take us three or four days to see them all, and the odds are that once we got somewhere, the enemy would be gone."

"Derek, you're thinking like a leg. We don't have to walk. Didn't they ever teach you not to walk when you could ride."

"Yes, sir."

"So we put the strikers on the choppers, fly them back to the fire base and let them off. Pick up the second lift and then break off lead for a scout. We can search those three villages in an hour. We see something, we land."

"Of course," said Kepler. "I'm not used to having choppers at my beck and call."

"Keep at it. You'll have the lead chopper once we get the men ferried around."

"Yes, sir."

Fetterman ran forward and tossed a grenade toward the front load. "Choppers inbound," he said unnecessarily.

Gerber glanced to the south and saw the approaching helicopters. He stood in the hot sun, watching them grow as the sound of the engines reached them.

"Nightfall," he said. "We should have them by nightfall."

15

WEST OF FIRE-SUPPORT
BASE CRAZY HORSE

The second lift landed, and Gerber ran over to the lead helicopter, which would become the scout again. Kepler was on the troop seat, a map in his lap. He was holding it down so that the wind caused by the rotor wash wouldn't rip it from his fingers and suck it out the door.

Gerber climbed up into the cargo compartment and crouched near him. Over the noise of the engine and the rotors, he yelled, "What's your itinerary?"

"Take them in order." He pointed to three sites on the map. "Near as I can tell, once they've hit here, they're going to head for Cambodia. If we missed them by much, we're not going to be able to find them."

"Especially if we don't find them by nightfall," said Gerber. "If they make it to night, they've got ten hours to fade away."

"I could leapfrog over to the last village first and work my way back here."

Gerber hesitated and then said, "No. Take them in order. And if you spot something, get out as fast as possible so you don't tip our hand."

"Yes, sir."

"You spend much more than an hour on the search and we're going to be fucked, because the choppers are going to have to refuel. At least yours will."

"As fast as I can, Captain. But I've got to see it all to make sure that we're not missing something important."

"You know what to do." Gerber slapped him on the knee and then jumped clear of the chopper.

Kepler sat there, sweating in the afternoon heat, and wished that he was somewhere else. He turned his attention to the map, marked the three enemy targets and then moved forward to talk to the pilots.

"Need to hit here, here and here," he shouted.

Rice turned in the seat and studied the map. He nodded and asked, "You have a way you want to do this?"

"What's that mean?"

"We can hit them high—two, three thousand feet, outside of small-arms range—and study the ground below, or we can scream across at fifty, sixty feet. A quick look, then turn a klick or so away and another look."

"Low and fast," said Kepler. "If I need a better look, you can pop on up, but if that happens, we'll be tipping our hands to the enemy."

"We'll do the best we can. Now, you ready?"

"I'm set."

Rice turned to face the front, and Kepler slipped back to the troop seat. As he sat down, the crew chief handed him a set of headphones that were plugged into the aircraft's avionics. There was a small black box that could be held in the palm of the hand so that Kepler could communicate with the pilots without having a hot mike.

"You set?" asked Rice again.

Kepler nodded and said, "Yes," but didn't hear his own voice. He pushed the button and repeated the word.

"Then we're on the go," said Rice.

They came up to a hover, held there for a moment and then began to slide forward. Rice held the nose up and held at three feet by easing the cyclic forward and pulling pitch. As they approached the trees, he came back with the cyclic, climbed up and then maintained his altitude, three or four feet above the trees. The airspeed continued to build until they were racing along and it was impossible to see anything except the greens of the trees as they flashed under him.

Moments later Rice announced, "Coming up on the first village. Slide over so that you'll be looking out the left side of the aircraft. Village will be there."

Kepler did as told and then wrapped his arm around the pole that supported the end of the troop seat. It was fastened to the deck and to the top, and Kepler felt better hanging on to it because it felt solid.

"Here we go," said Rice.

Kepler saw the edge of the village appear and then moved his eyes to the center of it. He saw a couple of people moving but they didn't look up. There was a fire burning, the smoke hanging low, near the ground. A farmer walked behind his water buffalo in a rice paddy. Everything seemed peaceful. There was no indication that the enemy was close.

"I've seen enough here," said Kepler.

"On to number two," said Rice.

Kepler leaned forward so that he could look back toward the village. There was one man standing at the edge of it, shaking his fist at the helicopter. Kepler laughed and waved back but he didn't think the man could see him.

"Number two," said Rice a few minutes later.

Kepler stared to the front, through the cargo compartment door. He saw the village in the distance. A conglomeration of hootches that had been built wherever a farmer had decided to put it. No pattern of streets at all. Crooked paths between the hootches. There were some fences woven from the thin branches of thorn-covered vines. There was a big stone oven at one end of the village. And there were people moving about.

As with the first ville, no one paid attention to them. The farmers in the rice fields continued their work without looking up. The women in the village, sitting outside their hootches and grinding grain, didn't look up. A couple of naked children stopped running around and looked up, but they didn't wave. They just watched as the helicopter flashed overhead.

"No," said Kepler. "I don't think there's anything going on here."

"On to number three," said Rice.

Kepler let go of the support and took out his map. The most likely route back to Cambodia would keep them in the forest for several klicks. If they weren't interested in a straight route, they could stay in forest and jungle most of the way, crossing the open areas at night. Kepler wouldn't be able to find them if they weren't in the third village. Not unless one of his agents saw something and managed to report it.

"Coming up on number three," said Rice.

"All set," said Kepler.

He shifted around and stared toward the front. He watched the village come up, but this time there were no people visible in it. The hootches looked to be in good repair, there was smoke from a cooking fire, but there were no people. No men out in the fields, no women attending the fires, and no children playing outside. It looked deserted.

"Swing around," said Kepler.

"Okay," said Rice.

As they flashed over the top, Kepler turned and watched as the village fell away. Near the center he thought he saw a body lying in the dirt, but then they were too far from the village and the angles were wrong.

"Anyone see anything?" asked Kepler.

"Seemed quiet," said Fallon. "No one around."

The crew chief agreed. "I didn't see a thing. No one down there."

They banked around. Kepler was looking straight at the jungle. Gravity forced him down into the seat. A pressure on his head and shoulders made him feel sick. They rolled out and in the bright afternoon sunlight, he could see the village spread out in front of him.

"Everyone look toward the center of it and tell me what you see there."

They came up to the village and this time Kepler knew right where to look. He saw one body lying on its side and another sprawled on its back. And that was all he saw.

"Got a body," said Rice.

"Two of them," said Fallon.

"Okay, that's got it," said Kepler. "Let's get the hell out of here. Straight to the south and then break back to the east toward the fire base."

"And then back here?" asked Rice.

"Of course."

"There wasn't much in the way of LZs around here," said Rice. "Paddies on the south with a tree line close, and that field on the west, again close to the ville and to the trees."

"That going to be a problem?"

"Not much of one."

"Can we talk to Captain Gerber?"

"Just have the crew chief flip your selector to position one. But remember, every time you push the button, you'll be on the air."

"Yes, sir."

The crew chief crawled around and moved the selector. Kepler pushed the button and said, "Zulu Six, Zulu Six, this is Zulu Two." He waited and then repeated the message.

Finally there was, "Go, Zulu Two."

Kepler was silent for a moment and then pushed his button. "Be advised we are inbound your location. Please be ready for transport."

There was a hesitation and then, "Understood. Six out."

Rice was on the radio then. "Hornet flight, let's wind them up. We'll be there in zero five."

"Roger."

To Kepler he said, "Flight will be ready when we get there."

Kepler nodded and then said, "Good." To himself, he added, "I wish I was."

THEY HAD HEARD the sound of the approaching helicopter long before it got there. Van knew what it meant. Even if they weren't looking for VC or NVA, when they flew over and saw them in the village, they would come back. The only thing Van could do was order everyone to hide. Immediately.

Van yelled his order. "Everyone inside. Now. Move it or die here. Inside."

For an instant no one moved. They stood rooted to the hot, red dirt. Then Van fired a shot into the ground. "Everyone inside," he repeated.

At first only two or three people moved, then finally everyone ran for the closest hootch. A dozen people tried to crowd through the door at once, all of them jammed together. Another man leaped at the pile and the logjam broke. The people tumbled into the hootch out of sight.

Van scrambled around so that he could see the sky outside. He lay in the shadows, looking up. He listened as the roar of the chopper got louder. He wished he had ordered his men not to fire at it. They were well-trained men who wouldn't break cover if ordered not to, good men who knew how to avoid being seen by the Americans. But now he was afraid that one of them would find the low-flying helicopter too tempting a target to ignore.

The helicopter shot by to the east, the skids barely above the trees there. In the bright sunlight, he could see the pilots sitting to the front. He could see the door gunner sitting behind his weapon, and he could see the single passenger. One man in jungle fatigues, holding on as if he were afraid he'd fall out.

In seconds the helicopter was gone, but Van knew how they operated. Sometimes they flew over and then came back a minute or two later to see if anything or anyone had moved. Catch the people in the open, thinking they were safe.

And just as he predicted, the helicopter came back. Again it was low and was overhead for only a few seconds. Van listened to the sound of it as it retreated the second time. He was sure that it wouldn't come back a third time. If it did, maybe they should shoot at it, because it meant the enemy was suspicious.

But it didn't return. The sound faded in the south and that was it. Van stood up and brushed the dust from the front of his uniform. He stepped out into the sunlight and squinted up at the sky. There was nothing to see and nothing to hear.

One of his soldiers appeared at his side. "Americans in a helicopter. Searching for someone."

"But not for us," said Van. "There was nothing for them to have seen here."

He glanced into the hootch and saw the faces of the people. Suddenly he realized his mistake. He had wanted to avoid contact with the Americans so he had hidden, but the peasants did not understand the military necessity of that. They had only seen his men fight for space in the hootches to hide from a single American aircraft. It appeared that Van and his squad of NVA soldiers were afraid.

"Everyone into the center of the village," he said. "Everyone there. Now."

"Yes, comrade."

"We must teach these peasants the power of the NVA and the importance of our mission."

He turned and stomped toward the center of the village. He stopped short and looked at the two bodies lying there, both partially in shadow. It seemed unlikely that the Americans in the helicopter had seen them, and if they had, it probably meant nothing to them. He should have had them picked up and moved before the helicopter appeared.

The villagers began to appear again, herded by his men. This time they did not ask the villagers to hurry. They demanded it, using their bayonets and rifle butts to convince them to move faster. They forced them into the center, in a huge cluster of men, women and children. Frightened people who sensed the anger of the soldiers but who didn't understand it. They knew that they would be lucky to survive the next hour.

Van moved through the crowd, glaring at them. He slapped a man and punched a woman, knocking her down to spit blood in the dirt. Children suddenly began to cry. Everyone knew that their lives hung by a narrow thread.

"The power of the NVA is immense. We come from the North to help the freedom-loving peoples of the South fight the imperialism of America and the oppression of puppet dictators in Saigon. We come because it is our duty to assist our brothers and sisters in the South. We do it because all Vietnamese people love freedom from oppression."

He stopped and looked into the faces of the people. He could see that they believed in his power. They had seen it earlier when he had shot the two villagers. But they didn't seem to believe anything else. They were there because he held the power in his hands. His men held the power in their hands.

"Our power is immense," he repeated. "We have fought the Americans in many fields and won many victories. We have faced them and defeated them. We are not afraid of them."

As he spoke those words he knew that he had pushed too far and said the wrong thing. The people had seen them diving into the dust at the approach of an American helicopter. They had seen Van and his men cower in the darkness of the huts while the Americans flew through the brightness of the afternoon. They had seen the Americans walking through the sunlight on many afternoons, while the VC and NVA only came at night, sneaking through the darkness like thieves. It was too late to convince the people of anything else.

Van shrugged then and walked to the edge of the group. He faced them for a moment. The only thing that he could do now was kill every one of them as a lesson to all those who lived elsewhere.

AS SOON AS Kepler's aircraft landed, Gerber ran out to it. He leaped into the back and yelled, "What did you see?"

"I think we've got them," he shouted back. He pointed to the map. "Here in number three."

"You see them?"

"No, sir. Saw no one, but there were two bodies in the center of the village."

"Then they've probably gone."

"No, sir. If they were gone the people would have been out. No, I think they're still there, in hiding. Heard the chopper and got out of the way before we could get there."

"Then let's go after them. What's the layout of the village like?"

Kepler explained it carefully, telling Gerber of the arrangement of the hootches, the proximity of the LZs and the trees. He laid it all out and then said, "If they're still in there, the LZ'll be hot."

Gerber nodded and turned. He slapped Rice on the shoulder and shouted, "Can we get guns in here?"

"Be an hour at best. Guns are tied up with the rest of the unit."

"Anyone available?"

"I'll check," said Rice, "but I wouldn't count on it."

"Do what you can." Gerber moved back to Kepler. "We hit the ground and we've got to move quickly into the village. We stay there in the rice paddy or that open field and we'll get cut up fast."

"Yes, sir."

"You assault the north end, I'll hit it in the middle and Tony'll bring the rest in toward the south. Move more or less on line and move quick, until we get under cover."

"Got it," said Kepler.

Rice waved at him. "No deal on the gunships. There's contact in the rubber plantation. Everyone's there. Couple of aircraft shot down. We'll play hell getting gun support."

"Shit," said Gerber.

Kepler shouted, "They'll be gone in an hour. Maybe less. They know we flew over. They'll finish their business and get the hell out."

"Rice, what about it?"

Fallon glared at the warrant officer and then shouted, "We shouldn't go without the gun support. Not into an area we know is hot."

"We don't get these guys now, we won't get them at all. They'll be gone," Gerber shouted.

Rice yelled, "We can go."

Gerber looked from the young warrant officer to the captain. The decision belonged to the senior officer. On the ground, and on matters that concerned the mission, the senior officer had to make the decision. But then, the chain of command in the aviation units was so screwy.

"Captain?" yelled Gerber.

For a moment Fallon was quiet, as if contemplating the situation, weighing the options and examining the plan. Then he nodded. "Yeah, let's do it."

Gerber nodded at Kepler and leaped from the rear of the helicopter. He ran back along the flight, waving an arm over his head, telling the other pilots to get ready for take off. He climbed into the rear of Chock Three and glanced out to the left. He saw the cloud of dust rise as the pilot pulled in pitch. The strikers left behind turned their backs to protect their eyes from the stinging dust.

The flight lifted off as one, but stayed close to the ground. They reached the trees, climbed, and then stayed low, as if trying to hide from the enemy. The airspeed increased as they raced along, the greens blurring.

There was a thrill to riding in a helicopter that was low-leveling. Somehow it seemed as if they were traveling faster than possible, roaring along toward the fight. Nothing could get to them if they stayed in the chopper. But then would come the sudden stop, the gravity pushing him down, and they would be out into a fight. Life and death. And yet, while low-leveling, the earth a blur, that didn't seem important.

"Five minutes," called the crew chief.

Gerber pulled the magazine from his weapon to check it, even though he knew it was fully loaded and seated properly. He jacked a round in the chamber and kept the barrel pointed up.

"Three minutes."

Now there wasn't time to think. Just time to react. Going in without arty prep and gun support. No arty because there were innocent people on the ground. No guns because the important war was somewhere else.

Gerber tried to think of something that he might have forgotten to say. Some important instruction that he hadn't relayed, but there was nothing. Kepler and Fetterman knew their jobs. If he hadn't told them something, they would think of it for themselves. Besides, the instant the first shot was fired, every plan was suddenly useless. They'd have to respond to the situation.

"One minute."

Gerber checked his straps and buckles. He slipped from the troop seat and knelt in the cargo compartment door on the side he thought would be facing the village. That way he could check the situation as he dived out the door.

Now it was up to the pilots to get them into the village. Get them on the ground so that they could begin the fight. Get them down before the enemy realized they were even close.

"Here we go."

Gerber hoped the enemy would be caught off guard.

But that ended in a burst of fire from an AK-47. Green tracers ripped by. And then a second and third burst, answered by a door gun. The fight had begun.

16

INBOUND TOWARD THE
NVA-HELD VILLAGE

Newhawser knew it was going to be a bad one. The enemy was supposed to be close and it was late in the afternoon. Charlie liked to shoot at helicopters late in the afternoon; there wouldn't be a big push to find him with night coming. And to make it worse, there was no gun support. Just the five slicks coming in, naked and unprotected.

"When we get close," said Newhawser, "you follow me on the controls."

"Of course," said Stockton.

To the crew chief and gunner he said, "There are friendlies in the village. Normal rules. You can fire if you identify the target."

"What about the tree line?"

"If we take any fire from there, hose it down. If not, just keep an eye on it."

"Yes, sir."

Then up ahead was the village. Mud hootches, some with thatched roofs and some with corrugated tin. An ox cart stood off to one side. There was a haystack and a water buffalo pen. The streets, or paths, meandered through the village, some lined by woven fences. Smoke from cooking fires hung low, close to the ground.

"Coming up on it," said Newhawser.

"Lead, you're in trail formation," said a voice on the radio.

"LZ is just ahead," said Rice in lead.

Then suddenly came a single burst of firing, an AK on full-auto.

"Flights taking fire on the right."

"Chock Three is taking fire."

"Got him spotted," yelled Hoskinson. There was an instant of silence and then Hoskinson lowered his voice and spoke calmly. "We have taken him under fire."

A second and then a third weapon opened up, the muzzle-flashes strobing from the doorway of hootches. M-60s began to hammer. Ruby-colored tracers slammed into the village. One of the enemy soldiers stopped shooting, but others joined in.

"Taking heavy fire on the right."

All the helicopter door guns were firing. Dirt around the hootch doors fountained as the 7.62 ammo struck. Clouds of dust swirled, but that didn't stop the enemy.

"Chock Three's taking hits."

"Roger, three."

"Shit! Four's going down. Lost the engine."

"Touching down now," yelled Rice. "Flare now!"

The flight suddenly stopped its forward progress. The noses of each of the aircraft came up and then dropped as the pilots leveled the skids. As one, the four aircraft touched the ground.

"Anyone see what happened to four?"

"Four's down," said Logan. "AC's wounded. We're getting the fuck out."

"Trail, can you pick them up?"

"Roger."

"Flight's still taking fire."

"Hang on," said Rice. "Give Trail some cover so that he can get the downed crew."

Over the intercom Fallon shouted, "We've got to get out of here. NOW!"

"Shut up," said Rice. "Davis, you keep firing into the muzzle-flashes."

The windshield seemed to explode then. There was a single quiet snap that sprayed Plexiglas across them. Then a half dozen more shattered the windshield.

"We're getting out," yelled Fallon. He grabbed collective and tried to jerk it up.

Rice leaned into it, holding it down. "Knock it off!" he shouted. "I've got it."

"Get us out of here," screamed Fallon.

"Ayres! Help me," shouted Rice. "Get him off the controls."

"You're down and unloaded," said Trail.

Rice ignored the message. He was trying to keep Fallon from jerking the controls and flipping the aircraft. Then Ayres was there, an arm locked under Fallon's chin, pulling up on his head. Fallon lost his grip on the cyclic.

"We're ready," said Trail.

Rice checked the instruments. Everything was in the green. He pulled pitch and said, "Lead's on the go."

"You're off with four. Fucking fire from the right. One ship down in the LZ."

There were questions that Rice wanted to ask but didn't. He had to concentrate on getting out of the LZ and then worry about wounds to pilots and the situation on the ground.

And he wanted to beat the shit out of Fallon. Rice figured it was bad enough to have to sit in his Plexiglas world and let the enemy take potshots at him. He didn't need Fallon making it almost impossible to survive.

"Clear of the LZ," said Trail. "Flight is joined."

THE NOSE OF THE AIRCRAFT came up violently and Gerber was thrown off balance. But then it leveled and sank to the foot-high grass. Gerber leaped from it, landed and ran forward five or six yards. He dived into the grass, the rotor wash tearing at his fatigues, the sound of the turbine filling the air.

All around him the same thing was happening. Men jumping from the helicopters. The door guns fell silent but the NVA kept firing. As the men cleared the fields of fire, the M-60s opened up. Rounds poured out and into the village.

For a moment everything hung there like that. Firing from the village. Firing from the helicopters. The sporadic firing from the strikers as they began to put out rounds.

Then the helicopters lifted off. The flight raced away toward the north, disappearing in seconds. A veil of silence seemed to fall and then lift as more of the strikers and the NVA began to shoot at each other. Tracers snapped overhead, green lancing from the village, and red pouring into it.

Gerber fired a short burst at the muzzle-flash in a darkened doorway, and then leaped to his feet. He waved a hand and yelled, "Let's go." He started running, right and then left and finally diving for cover. Machine-gun bullets snapped by him. A striker running behind him was hit, and fell into the grass. Another tried to reach the downed man, but was forced to take cover himself.

To his right, Fetterman was sprinting toward the village. The master sergeant reached a hootch and dived for cover at the base of the wall. He rolled to his back, pulled the pin from a grenade and tossed it through the window. Without hesitation he rolled against the wall, burying his face against it. The explosion shook the thatch of the roof and blew a hole in one mud wall. Fetterman got up and disappeared into the hootch as the smoke boiled out the door.

Gerber was up and running again. He reached the village and crouched near the mud wall of a hootch. There was firing around him. AKs and M-16s. People were shouting, screaming. Men, women and children.

For a moment Gerber couldn't see any enemy soldiers. He heard the firing to the right and left. He heard commands in Vietnamese, but couldn't see who was giving them.

He moved around a corner, keeping to the shadow at the side of the hootch. He reached the end and stopped. There was sudden movement in front of him. Raising his weapon, he aimed, but didn't fire.

A kid ran out. A small boy in black shorts. His eyes were closed as if he didn't want to see what was happening around him. He ran into a patch of sunlight, stopped and started to scream. Bullets kicked up dust around him.

Gerber sprinted from cover, snagged the kid around the waist and dived over a woven fence and into the front yard of a hootch. The kid screamed with fear and surprise. Gerber hung on to him. He glanced at the hootch and pushed the boy toward the door. He fell to his stomach and continued to wail.

Gerber moved around so that he could look over the top of the fence. A single man ran from one corner of a hootch to the door of another. He stood in the doorway, and sprayed the inside with AK fire.

Gerber aimed at him and squeezed the trigger three times quickly. The first round missed but the second caught the man as he was beginning to turn. It hit his shoulder, spinning him. He fell back against the mud of the hootch, blood staining it and his arm. The last round punched into his chest. He stood for a moment, coughing blood, and then doubled over, falling facedown in the dirt.

Two strikers ran from cover toward the downed NVA. One covered as the other checked the body. He grabbed the AK and then went into the hootch.

Slowly they were all working their way into the village.

VAN WAS STANDING in front of the crowd of villagers, wanting to watch them all die in the dirt when the sound of the choppers came again. Not a lone craft this time but a small flight. He, along with the members of the squad, turned to face the south. Squinting into the late-afternoon sun, they saw the helicopters, looking like giant omnivorous insects.

As he turned to yell, the villagers suddenly scattered. It was as if some unheard command had been given. They knew that they had one chance for life and they took it.

Van dropped to one knee and opened fire with his AK. He emptied a magazine into the fleeing villagers, killing men, women and children. He didn't care who he hit and killed. In fact he wanted to kill them all.

With the villagers trying to hide, Van pointed at the sky. "We shoot down the helicopters. Kill the Americans."

The men ran for the edge of the village where the American helicopters were landing. One man opened fire with his AK. That was returned. Then more of the men began to shoot. Even in the sunlight, Van could see the tracers.

For a moment he stood near the center of the village, looking down at the bodies of the dead. A dozen people lay sprawled in the dirt. Van walked among them, almost like a man on a Sunday stroll, shooting each person in the back of the head to make sure that none of them survived.

Firing from the edge of the village increased. M-16s joined in. The helicopters took off to the north out of the danger zone.

One of his men ran back, yelling, "The Americans are coming. They've landed."

"Control yourself," snapped Van. "There can't be that many of them. Kill them."

The man looked around wildly and then half turned. "Go. Help your comrades!" ordered Van. "Death to the Americans."

The man whirled and ran back the way he'd come. Van slipped to the east, away from the approaching Americans. He stopped in the shadow of a tree. Glancing to the right, he saw several villagers inside a hootch. He raised his weapon and sprayed the doorway, driving them back and killing two of them.

He was up and running then. He reached the edge of the village on the side opposite the Americans. There was no need to hurry. Not with his men fighting and dying. All he had to do was cross the open rice paddies and escape into the jungle. The Americans would never find him there. Not with night coming. They'd be too busy mopping up the resistance and then trying to help the wounded. Safety lay just over a hundred yards away, in the trees.

He raised the back of his hand to his lips. They were dry, and the rest of his body was wet with sweat. He glanced to the rear, where the battle was being fought, and wondered if he should spring across the open ground immediately or if he should wait and do it in pieces.

FETTERMAN EXITED THE HOOTCH that he had grenaded. The body of a single NVA soldier lay on the dirt floor. The master sergeant stripped the weapon and ammo pouch from him, tossing them out the door. Leaving the body where it fell, obviously dead, he followed the weapon. He knelt there, listened to the flow of the battle and then ran to join it.

As he came around the corner of the hootch, he spotted one man near a tree, firing at the strikers. One striker lay face-down in the dirt, his weapon a foot from him. Two others were shooting at the NVA soldier.

Fetterman aimed and pulled the trigger. The round hit the man in the head, throwing him over on his side. His weapon flew out of his hands as he died. When he fell, the strikers were up and running. One of them leaped over the body, spun and pumped a half dozen shots into it.

Fetterman left them to their fun. He ran along the side of a hootch. He stopped once and wiped the sweat from his face. He was about to step around the corner when one of the NVA came from the other direction. The man stopped dead in his tracks and pulled the trigger of his AK almost in reflex. The bullet struck the ground five feet from Fetterman.

Fetterman responded by kicking the man. He tumbled to the left and tried to raise his rifle. Fetterman kicked it out of his hand and then punched him once in the face. The man's eyes glazed and his head lolled.

"Prisoner," shouted Fetterman.

A striker ran to him. Fetterman pointed and said, "I have a prisoner. I don't want him to die. You guard him."

The striker nodded and Fetterman ran off. He searched the far side of the village and slid to a halt. He turned and looked back but there was nothing to see there except two dead strikers and the dead NVA by the tree.

He crouched and surveyed the area, waiting for something else to happen.

NHU HAD TAKEN a position in a hootch, looking out the window. He'd kicked apart a small wooden cabinet made from scrap lumber and stomped on the small battery-powered radio. He listened to the helicopters land and heard the firing begin. He watched the villagers run by him toward where they thought they would find safety. Even though Van had ordered them to kill everyone, Nhu didn't shoot them. They were unarmed. They were women and children and shouldn't be murdered.

Instead he waited for the hated Americans to appear. He stood well back in the shadows of the hootch so that even the barrel of his weapon wouldn't be visible in the sunlight. Two of his comrades ran past, one of them without a weapon.

Then a Vietnamese soldier appeared. A short dark man wearing a striped uniform and carrying an M-16. Nhu aimed at the man and fired. He missed, but the man seemed unaware of the situation. Nhu fired again and the man fell to the ground, scrambling toward the door of a hootch.

Nhu fired again and again, but the shot was always off. Dirt kicked up behind the striker. A cloud of it seemed to follow him as he moved faster and faster, finally losing his weapon in his haste. After the man gained the safety of the hootch, Nhu waited for him, but he didn't reappear.

Then men were running around him, firing at each other. A man fell, the blood exploding from his body. A second died as his head disintegrated. A striker dived for cover and then popped up firing his weapon on full-auto. He held the trigger down until he was out of ammo and then disappeared again.

There was a thud against the side of the hootch. Nhu dived for cover and was rocked by an explosion. Dirt shook from the thatch and filled the air. His ears rang with the flat bang of the detonation. He tasted dirt and for an instant wasn't sure what happened.

A man threw himself into the hootch with Nhu. He fired, the weapon's strobing lighting the interior of the hootch in yellow fire. Bullets ricocheted. There was breaking glass. Nhu rolled to his side and felt a pain there. He tried to sit up but the room turned black and he fell.

The man fired again and Nhu saw his silhouette. Suddenly he wanted nothing more than to be left alone. He pushed his AK out and lifted it, pulling the trigger as he did. The weapon jerked itself out of his hand, but the enemy soldier was shoved backward out the door.

With the enemy gone, Nhu crashed into the corner. He pushed the bamboo mat out of the way and discovered the family bunker. That could provide safety for him if he could get it out. He tried to sit up and failed. He tried to jerk the trapdoor out of the way but didn't have the strength. For a moment he lay there, wishing he could get out. And then the shade of black started down, covering his eyes, and he had no more wishes.

GERBER RAN THROUGH the center of the village. He found the bodies of the dead Vietnamese, but didn't stop. The odor of copper was heavy in the air. It overpowered the stench of the water buffalo pen and the open sewer. The blood was thick and the flies were already beginning to gather. The battle wasn't over and the flies had already found the dead.

He continued on. The firing was tapering and now sporadic as the resistance was wiped out. He found a striker lying on his side, blood pooling under him. Part of his jaw had been shot away, and his eyes were open, staring. His weapons were gone. An NVA soldier had killed him and taken his equipment.

Gerber continued to move, coming to a broken-down mud fence. He stopped there for a moment. Suddenly he was aware of his heart hammering in his chest. He was sweaty and his muscles ached. It was the good life in Saigon. No time for a gym or workouts. Time for big meals and lots of sleep.

Ignoring the physical pain, he pushed himself forward. There was a shot that hit the top of the wall, spraying him with dried mud and dirt. He dropped to the ground and rolled behind the wall. He had no idea where the shot had come from.

He crawled to the end of the wall and saw a single NVA soldier who fired at Gerber and then got up to run. Gerber returned fire. As did half a dozen strikers. The man was hit, lifted from his feet and thrown to the ground. He rolled over and over, then tried to stand up. He got to his knees and then fell forward, not moving again.

Firing died, then. Single shots in the distance. Gerber got to his feet and moved to the edge of the village. He saw Fetterman and headed toward the master sergeant.

"Think that's got it."

Fetterman nodded. "We're going to need medics. Lots of wounded."

"I'll find the RTO."

"Yes, sir."

Movement in the rice paddies to the east caught their attention. Both dived for cover. Gerber jerked his rifle around and saw the AK carried by the fleeing man. He aimed and fired, as did Fetterman.

For a moment it looked as if they had both missed. Then the man stumbled. He continued to run in an uncoordinated fashion, his arms outflung. He dropped his rifle but didn't seem to care about that. Finally he fell to the side, over the edge of a rice paddy dike. There was a splash of muddy water and then no more movement.

"Now that's got it," said Gerber.

"Yes, sir. I'll get a sweep organized. Pick up the weapons and check on the wounded."

"And the villagers," said Gerber. "Too bad we can't get the newspapers out here to see the dead Vietnamese villagers."

"Hell, sir, they'd just blame us."

Gerber shrugged. "I suppose you're right."

"Anything else?"

Gerber shook his head. "Have Kepler check it out, but I think we got that assassination squad."

"That's something, anyway," said Fetterman.

"That's probably as good as it's going to get," said Gerber. He wished there was something more he could do, but had no idea what it could be. He turned from the rice paddy and started back toward the center of the village. It seemed anticlimactic.

17

THE CARASEL HOTEL, SAIGON

The food sitting in front of Gerber was untouched. He had been hungry when he sat down, but as he drank the wine that Fetterman ordered at Morrow's insistence, he lost his appetite. It was thinking about the scene at the village and the response of those who supposedly cared about such things.

"I didn't know that news had a shelf life," said Gerber.

Morrow, who had heard the story after Gerber had been debriefed, shrugged. "What can I tell you? We all have perceptions about what is important. To the people back home, Vietnamese killing Vietnamese doesn't seem as important as Americans killing Vietnamese."

"We talk about an informed electorate. We talk about objective reporting and unbiased accounts, but then we have a censorship that keeps the public from knowing what's really happening here."

"There's only so much space in the paper and only so many minutes on a broadcast," said Morrow. She put down her fork and picked up her wine.

Gerber sat there, thinking about the past few hours. They had determined that the men they had found in the village were the assassins sent from the North. The single prisoner they had taken told them that. He had also told them that their leader had exceeded his orders by shooting the people.

They had stayed at the village until a company of infantry soldiers from fire-support base Crazy Horse arrived. They had brought medical aid, food and supplies and had worked at getting the people out of their hootches for treatment.

The wounded had been airlifted to the hospitals, and then Gerber, Fetterman and Kepler had been flown back to Saigon. Kepler had opted to stay at the SOG building while Gerber and Fetterman went over to MACV. There they had met with General Petrak again. They told him what they had seen and what they had done.

Petrak had nodded as he listened and then asked, "You're sure you got the assassins?"

"Sergeant Kepler went through the documentation. We're sure."

"Where are the papers?" asked Petrak.

"Sergeant Kepler has them over at the SOG building at Tan Son Nhut. He and several other Intel types are checking it out closely."

"When they're finished, I'd like to see their report."

"Certainly, General."

There was a silence then as Petrak glanced at a report in front of him. "If that's all," he said.

"Just the problem with the South Vietnamese," said Gerber.

"Fuck 'em," said Petrak. "If the South Vietnamese would fight for themselves, we wouldn't have to be here."

"We're talking about farmers and women and children. They're not soldiers."

"Fuck 'em anyway," said Petrak. "If there's nothing else, then you can go."

Gerber had left then. With Fetterman, he had driven downtown and found Morrow. Gerber had given her the story, but her boss had said the same thing. "Fuck 'em."

When they failed to interest the press, Fetterman suggested they eat dinner. Gerber decided that it wouldn't solve the problem, but it wouldn't hurt it either.

So they had gone up to the hotel restaurant and ordered, and then Gerber lost his appetite. And nothing Fetterman or Morrow could say could help.

Morrow put her glass of wine down. "You can't change the world."

"I don't know," said Gerber. "I guess I could accept the press failing to be interested in what we found, but the Army shouldn't ignore it. The terror tactics of the NVA could be exploited and turned against them, but no one wants to think that far ahead. We bring—" Gerber shook his head. "I'm beginning to sound like Sergeant Fetterman. A solution to every problem."

"You can't complain," said Fetterman, "unless you can offer an intelligent solution to the problem you're complaining about."

"I could give you a typewritten list of various solutions," said Gerber.

"Then you may complain all you want, though telling me about it sure won't help."

Morrow leaned over and grabbed her purse. "Hey, I got some good news today." She plucked a letter from it and waved it. "It's from my mother. You'll never guess what happened."

"You won the Pulitzer Prize."

"Even better," said Morrow. "Karen's wedding didn't come off." She laughed. "The great doctor left her standing at the altar. He closed his office and moved out of town. She was beside herself."

Gerber picked up his glass of wine and drank deeply. "Maybe there is a little justice in the world after all."

NEWHAWSER SAT IN THE officers' club at Cu Chi and shook his head. "Not fair," he said. "I was all set for three or four weeks of living in Saigon. Hell, I was promised that. Then close my flight records and I'm back in the World to teach warrant officer candidates how to fly at Fort Wolters." He waved a hand. "Now look at where I am."

Rice sat there and downed a bourbon on the rocks. "At least you weren't flying with a fucking coward."

"What are you going to do about that?" said Newhawser.

Rice shrugged. "Forget it, I guess. First time under fire. Everyone gets one chance to screw up. But I'll keep an eye on him. It happens again and he's gone."

"So," said Newhawser, "we're back to my problem. My stolen three weeks in Saigon."

"What d'you want?" asked Rice. "You got to see Tu Do Street, you got thrown in jail, and we stole that whore from some Marine or staff sergeant or some damn thing."

"True."

"And all you got was hung over. I got the clap."

"That's what you get for fucking around. All alcohol does is kill brain cells."

Rice went to the bar, got another bourbon and came back. He sat down and said, "It was interesting, though."

"Very."

"One of the few times that I've been on a mission where it seemed that the men running it had any idea what was going on. We did well."

"Logan did real well getting Cramer out of the chopper. And Cramer did real well. Hurt bad enough to get out of here, close enough to the end of his tour that he doesn't have to come back, but not hurt bad enough to be fucked up for the rest of his miserable life.''

Again Rice downed his drink in one quick swallow. ''We all did well.''

''But the whole thing sucks,'' said Newhawser. ''We fly the missions, destroy the enemy, and the next day we have to do it all over again. We make no progress.''

''You going to be this way all night?''

Newhawser nodded. ''Yeah, I think so.''

''Then there's only one thing to do,'' said Rice looking at his empty glass.

''What's that?''

''Get drunk.''

''A good plan. Let's do it.''

GLOSSARY

AC—An aircraft commander. The pilot in charge of the aircraft.

ADO—An A-detachment's area of operations.

ADF—Automatic Direction Finding. An aircraft radio-navigational aid.

AFVN—The Armed Forces radio and television network in Vietnam. Army PFC Pat Sajak was probably the most memorable of AFVN's DJs with his loud and long, "GOOOOOOOOOOOOOD MORNing, Vietnam." The spinning Wheel of Fortune gives no clues about his whereabouts today.

AGGRESSOR FATIGUES—Black fatigues called aggressor fatigues because they are the color of the uniforms worn by the aggressors during war games in the World during training.

AIT—Advanced Individual Training. The school soldiers were sent to after Basic.

AK-47—Assault rifle normally used by the North Vietnamese and the Vietcong.

ANGRY-109—AN-109, the radio used by the Special Forces for long-range communications.

AO—Area of operations.

AO DAI—A long, dresslike garment, split up the sides and worn over pants.

AP—Air Police. The old designation for the guards on Air Force bases. Now referred to as security police.

AP Rounds—Armor-piercing ammunition.

APU—Auxiliary power unit. An outside source of power used to start aircraft engines.

ARC LIGHT—The term used for a B-52 bombing mission. Also known as heavy arty.

ARVN—Army of the Republic of Vietnam. A South Vietnamese soldier. Also known as Marvin Arvin.

ASA—Army Security Agency.

ASH AND TRASH—Refers to helicopter support missions that did not involve a direct combat role. They were hauling supplies, equipment, mail and all sorts of ash and trash.

AST—The control officer between the men in isolation and the outside world. He is responsible for taking care of all problems.

AUTOVON—An Army phone system that allows soldiers on base to call another base, bypassing the civilian phone system.

BDA—Bomb damage assessment. The official report on how well the bombing mission went.

BIG RED ONE—The nickname of the First Infantry Division. It came from the shoulder patch that contained a big, red numeral one.

BISCUIT—C-rations.

BODY COUNT—The number of enemy killed, wounded or captured during an operation. Used by Saigon and Washington as a means of measuring progress of the war.

BOOM-BOOM—Term used by the Vietnamese prostitutes in selling their product.

BOONDOGGLE—Any military operation that hasn't been completely thought out. An operation that is ridiculous.

BOONIE HATS—A soft cap worn by the grunts in the field when they were not wearing their steel pot.

BROWNING M-2—Fifty-caliber machine gun manufactured by Browning.

BROWNING M-35—The automatic pistol, a 9 mm weapon, that became the favorite of the Special Forces.

BUSHMASTER—A jungle warfare expert or soldier skilled in jungle navigation. Also a large deadly snake not common to Vietnam but mighty tasty.

C AND C—The Command and Control aircraft that circled overhead to direct the combined air and ground operations.

CA—Combat Assault.

CAO BOIS—(cowboys) A term that referred to the criminals of Saigon who rode motorcycles.

CARIBOU—Cargo transport plane.

CHECKRIDE—A flight in which a pilot checks the proficiency of another. It can be an informal review of the various techniques or a very formal test of a pilot's knowledge.

CHINOOK—Army Aviation twin-engine helicopter. A CH-47. Also known as SHIT HOOK.

CHOCK—Refers to the number of the aircraft in the flight. Chock Three is the third, Chock Six is the sixth.

CLAYMORE—An antipersonnel mine that fires seven hundred and fifty steel balls with a lethal range of fifty meters.

CLOSE AIR SUPPORT—Use of airplanes and helicopters to fire on enemy units near friendlies.

CO CONG—Term referring to the female Vietcong.

COLT—A Soviet-built small transport plane. The NATO code name for Soviet and Warsaw Pact transports all begin with the letter C.

CONEX—A steel container about ten feet high, ten feet wide and ten feet long, used to haul equipment and supplies.

DAC CONG—The sappers who attack in the front ranks to blow up the wire so that the infantry can assault the camp.

DAI UY—Vietnamese army rank, the equivalent of captain.

DEROS—Date of estimated return from overseas.

DIRNSA—Director, National Security Agency.

E AND E—Escape and evasion.

FEET WET—Term used by pilots to describe flight over water.

FIELD GRADE—Refers to officers above the rank of captain, but under that of brigadier general. In other words, majors, lieutenant colonels and colonels.

FIRECRACKER—A special artillery shell that explodes into a number of small bomblets to detonate later. It is the artillery version of the cluster bomb and was a secret weapon employed tactically for the first time in Khe Sanh.

FIREFLY—A helicopter with a battery of bright lights mounted in or on it. The aircraft is designed to draw enemy fire at night so that gunships, orbiting close by, can attack the target.

FIRST SHIRT—A military term referring to the first sergeant.

FIVE—Radio call sign for the executive officer of a unit.

FOB—Forward operating base.

FOX MIKE—FM radio.

FNG—Fucking new guy.

FREEDOM BIRD—Name given to any aircraft that took troops out of Vietnam. Usually referred to the commercial jet flights that took men back to the World.

GARAND—The M-1 rifle that was replaced by the M-14. Issued to the Vietnamese early in the war.

GO-TO-HELL RAG—Towel or any large cloth worn around the neck by grunts.

GRAIL—The NATO name for the shoulder-fired SA-7 surface-to-air missile.

GUARD THE RADIO—A term that means standing by in the commo bunker and listening for messages.

GUIDELINE—The NATO name for the SA-2 surface-to-air missiles.

GUNSHIP—Armed helicopter or cargo plane that carries weapons instead of cargo.

HE—High-explosive ammunition.

HOOTCH—Almost any shelter, from temporary to long-term.

HORN—Term that referred to a specific kind of radio operations that used satellites to rebroadcast the messages.

HORSE—See BISCUIT.

HOTEL THREE—A helicopter landing area at Saigon's Tan Son Nhut Airport.

HUEY—A UH-1 helicopter.

HUMINT—A human Intelligence resource. In other words, they talked to someone who gave them the information.

ICS—The official name of the intercom system in an aircraft.

IN-COUNTRY—Term used to refer to American troops operating in South Vietnam. They were all in-country.

INTELLIGENCE—Any information about enemy operations. It can include troop movements, weapons capabilities, biographies of enemy commanders, and general information about terrain features. It is any information that would be useful in planning a mission.

KA-BAR—A type of military combat knife.

KIA—Killed in action. (Since the U.S. was not engaged in a declared war, the use of the term KIA was not authorized. KIA came to mean enemy dead. Americans were KHA or killed in hostile action.)

KLICK—A thousand meters. A kilometer.

LIMA LIMA—Land line. Refers to telephone communications between two points on the ground.

LLDB—Luc Luong Dac Biet. The South Vietnamese Special Forces. Sometimes referred to as the Look Long, Duck Back.

LOW QUARTERS—Military term for regular shoes. In the case of the Army, it means the black dress shoes worn with the Class A and Dress uniforms.

LP—Listening Post. A position outside the perimeter manned by a couple of people to give advance warning of enemy activity.

LRRP—Long-range reconnaissance patrol.

LSA—A lubricant used by soldiers on their weapons to ensure they would continue to operate properly.

LZ—Landing zone.

M-3A1—Also known as a Grease Gun. A .45-caliber submachine gun that was favored in World War Two by the GIs because its slow rate of fire meant that the barrel didn't rise and they didn't burn through their ammo as fast as they did in some of the other weapons.

M-14—Standard rifle of the U.S., eventually replaced by the M-16. It fired the standard NATO round—7.62 mm.

M-16—Became the standard infantry weapon of the Vietnam War. It fired 5.56 mm ammunition.

M-79—A short-barrel, shoulder-fired weapon that fires a 40 mm grenade. These can be high-explosive, white phosphorus or canister.

M-113—The numerical designation of an armored personnel carrier.

MACV—Military Assistance Command, Vietnam, replaced MAAG in 1964.

MAD MINUTE—A specified time on a base camp when the men in the bunkers would clear their weapons. It came to mean the random firing of all the camp's weapons just as fast as everyone could shoot.

MATCU—Marine Air Traffic Control Unit.

MEDEVAC—Also called Dustoff. Helicopter used to take the wounded to the medical facilities.

MI—Military Intelligence.

MIA—Missing in action.

MONOPOLY MONEY—A term used by the servicemen in Vietnam to describe the MPC handed out in lieu of regular U.S. currency.

MOS—Military Occupation Specialty. A job description.

MPC—Military Payment Certificates. The Monopoly money used instead of real cash.

NCO—A noncommissioned officer. A noncom. A sergeant.

NCOIC—NCO in charge. The senior NCO in a unit, detachment or a patrol.

NDB—Nondirectional beacon. A radio beacon that can be used for homing.

NEXT—The man who was the next to be rotated home. See SHORT.

NINETEEN—The average age of the combat soldier in Vietnam, as opposed to twenty-six in World War II.

NOUC MAM—A pungent sauce used by the Vietnamese.

NVA—The North Vietnamese Army. Also used to designate a soldier from North Vietnam.

ONTOS—A Marine weapon that consisted of six 106 mm recoilless rifles mounted on a tracked vehicle.

ORDER OF BATTLE—A listing of the units available and to be used during the battle. It is not necessarily a list of how or when the units will be used, but a listing of who and what could be used.

P (PIASTER)—The basic monetary unit in South Vietnam, worth slightly less than a penny.

PETA-PRIME—A black, tarlike substance that melted in the heat of the day to become a sticky black nightmare that clung to boots, clothes and equipment. Used to hold down the dust during the dry season.

PETER PILOT—The copilot in a helicopter.

PLF—Parachute landing fall. The roll used by parachutists on landing.

POL—Petroleum, oil and lubricants. The refueling point on many military bases.

POW—Prisoner of war.

PRC-10—Portable radio.

PRC-25—A lighter radio that replaced the PRC-10.

PULL PITCH—Term used by helicopter pilots that means they are going to take off.

PUNJI STAKE—Sharpened bamboo hidden to penetrate the foot. Sometimes dipped in feces.

PUZZLE PALACE—A term referring to the Pentagon. It was called the puzzle palace because no one knew what was going on in it. The Puzzle Palace East referred to MACV or USARV Headquarters in Saigon.

PVT—A setting on the radio control head in a helicopter that allowed the pilots to converse without the others listening in.

RED LEGS—A term that refers to the artillerymen. It comes from the old Army where the artillerymen wore a red stripe on the legs of their uniforms.

REMF—A rear-echelon motherfucker.

RINGKNOCKER—Graduate of a military academy. The term refers to the ring worn by all graduates.

RLO—Real live officer. A term used by warrant officers to refer to officers who were commissioned.

RON—Remain overnight. Term used by flight crews to indicate a flight that would last longer than a day.

RPD—Soviet-made light machine gun, 7.62 mm.

RTO—Radio telephone operator. The radio man of a unit.

RUFF-PUFFS—A term applied to the RF-PFs, of the regional forces and popular forces. Militia drawn from the local population.

S-3—The company-level operations officer. The same as the G-3 on a general's staff.

SA-2—A surface-to-air missile fired from a fixed site. It is a radar-guided missile nearly thirty-five feet long.

SA-7—A surface-to-air missile that is shoulder-fired and infrared homing.

SACSA—Special Assistant for Counterinsurgency and Special Activities.

SAFE AREA—Selected area for evasion. It doesn't mean that the area is safe from the enemy, only that the terrain, location or local population make the area a good place for escape and evasion.

SAM TWO—A reference to the SA-2 Guideline.

SAR—Search and Rescue. SAR forces would be the people involved in search and rescue missions.

SECDEF—Secretary of Defense.

SHORT-TIME—A GI term for a quickie.

SHORT-TIMER—Person who had been in Vietnam for nearly a year and who would be rotated back to the World soon. When his DEROS was the shortest in the unit, the person was said to be next.

SINGLE DIGIT MIDGET—A soldier with fewer than ten days left in-country.

SIX—Radio call sign for the unit commander.

SKS—Soviet-made carbine.

SMG—Submachine gun.

SOI—Signal operating instructions. The booklet that contained the call signs and radio frequencies of the units in Vietnam.

SOP—Standard operating procedure.

SPIKE TEAM—Special Forces team made up for a direct action mission.

STEEL POT—The standard U.S. Army helmet. The steel pot was the outer, metal cover.

TAOR—Tactical area of operational responsibility.

TEAM UNIFORM OR COMPANY UNIFORM—UHF radio frequency on which the team or the company communicates. Frequencies were changed periodically in an attempt to confuse the enemy.

THREE—Radio call sign of the operations officer.

THREE CORPS—The military area around Saigon. Vietnam was divided into four corps areas.

TOC—Tactical operations center.

TO&E—Table of organization and equipment. A detailed listing of all the men and equipment that are assigned to a unit.

TOT—Time over target. It refers to the time that the aircraft are supposed to be over the drop zone with the parachutists, or the target if the planes are bombers.

TRICK CHIEF—NCOIC for a shift.

TRIPLE A—Antiaircraft artillery or AAA. This is anything used to shoot at airplanes and helicopters.

TWO—Radio call sign of the Intelligence officer.

TWO-OH-ONE (201) FILE—The military records file that listed all a soldier's qualifications, training, experience and abilities. It was passed from unit to unit so that the new commander would have some idea about the capabilities of the incoming soldier.

UMZ—Ultramilitarized Zone. It was the name GIs gave to the DMZ (Demilitarized Zone).

UNIFORM—Refers to the UHF radio. Company Uniform would be the frequency assigned to that company.

USARV—United States Army, Vietnam.

VC—Vietcong, called Victor Charlie (phonetic alphabet), or just Charlie.

VIETCONG—A contraction of Vietnam Cong San (Vietnamese Communist).

VIET CONG SAN—The Vietnamese Communists. A term in use since 1956.

WHITE MICE—Referred to the South Vietnamese military police because they all wore white helmets.

WIA—Wounded in action.

WILLIE PETE—WP, White phosphorus, called smoke rounds. Also used as antipersonnel weapons.

WOBBLY ONE—Refers to a W-1, the lowest of the warrant officer grades. Helicopter pilots who weren't commissioned started out as Wobbly Ones.

WORLD—The United States.

WSO—Weapons system officer. The name given to the man who rode in the back seat of a Phantom because he was responsible for the weapons systems.

XO—Executive officer of a unit.

X-RAY—A term that refers to an engineer assigned to a unit.

ZAP—To ding, pop caps or shoot. To kill.

A ruthless mercenary threatens global stability.

DON PENDLETON's

MACK BOLAN®

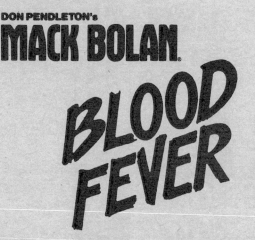

BLOOD FEVER

A renegade mercenary calling himself the Major has been dealing in nuclear weapons manufactured with stolen technology and kidnapped scientists.

On a terrorist recon mission in Colorado, Bolan taps into the munitions dealer's global organization.

Now, one man's war against terrorism is about to put the death merchant out of business.

The line between good and evil is a tightrope no man should walk. Unless that man is the Executioner.

BLOWOUT $3.95 ☐
Framed for murder and wanted by both sides of the law, Bolan
escapes into the icy German underground to stalk a Mafia-
protected drug baron.

TIGHTROPE $3.95 ☐
When top officials of international Intelligence agencies are
murdered, Mack Bolan pits his skill against an alliance of
renegade agents and uncovers a deadly scheme to murder the
U.S. President.

MOVING TARGET $3.95 ☐
America's most powerful corporations are reaping huge profits
by dealing in arms with anyone who can pay the price. Dogged
by assassins, Mack Bolan becomes caught in a power struggle
that might be his last.

FLESH & BLOOD $3.95 ☐
When Asian communities are victimized by predators among
their own—thriving gangs of smugglers, extortionists and
pimps—they turn to Mack Bolan for help.

Total Amount	$ _____
Plus 75¢ Postage	.75
Payment enclosed	$ _____

Please send a check or money order payable to Gold Eagle Books.

In the U.S.	In Canada
Gold Eagle Books	Gold Eagle Books
901 Fuhrmann Blvd.	P.O. Box 609
Box 1325	Fort Erie, Ontario
Buffalo, NY 14269-1325	L2A 5X3

Please Print
Name: _____
Address: _____
City: _____
State/Prov: _____
Zip/Postal Code: _____

GOLD EAGLE®

SMB-3

ABLE TEAM

DICK STIVERS

Action writhes in the reader's own streets as Able Team's Carl "Ironman" Lyons, Pol Blancanales and Gadgets Schwarz make triple trouble in blazing war. Join Dick Stivers's Able Team as it returns to the United States to become the country's finest tactical neutralization squad in an era of urban terror and unbridled crime.

"Able Team will go anywhere, do anything, in order to complete their mission. Plenty of action! Recommended!"
—West Coast Review of Books

Able Team titles are available wherever paperbacks are sold.

GOLD EAGLE

AT-1R

Take 4 explosive books plus a mystery bonus FREE

Mail to **Gold Eagle Reader Service**

In the U.S.
P.O. Box 1394
Buffalo, N.Y. 14240-1394

In Canada
P.O. Box 609,
Fort Erie, Ont. L2A 5X3

YEAH! Rush me 4 free Gold Eagle novels and my free mystery bonus. Then send me 6 brand-new novels every other month as they come off the presses. Bill me at the low price of just $14.94— an 11% saving off the retail price - plus 95¢ postage and handling per shipment. There is no minimum number of books I must buy. I can always return a shipment and cancel at any time. Even if I never buy another book from Gold Eagle, the 4 free novels and the mystery bonus are mine to keep forever.   166 BPM BPS9

_____

Name   (PLEASE PRINT)

_____

Address   Apt. No.

_____

City   State/Prov.   Zip/Postal Code

_____

Signature (If under 18, parent or guardian must sign)

This offer is limited to one order per household and not valid to present subscribers Terms and prices subject to change without notice.   4E-AD1

Vietnam: Ground Zero is written by men who saw it all, did it all and lived to tell it all

"Some of the most riveting war fiction written..."
—Ed Gorman, *Cedar Rapids Gazette*

STRIKE $3.95 ☐
An elite Special Forces team is dispatched when heavy traffic in enemy supplies to Nui Ba Den has Intelligence in Saigon worried. Primed for action, Mack Gerber and his men wage a firefight deep inside a mountain fortress, while the VC outside are poised for a suicide raid against an American political delegation.

SHIFTING FIRES $3.95 ☐
An American Special Forces squad is assembled to terminate a renowned general suspected of directing operations at the siege of Khe Sanh, where six thousand U.S. troops are pinned down by NVA regulars.

THE RAID $3.95 ☐
The Pentagon calls in experts in unconventional warfare when a Soviet training contingent is discovered in North Vietnam. Their mission: attack and kill every Russian in the place... and get out alive.

Total Amount	$	_____
Plus 75¢ Postage		.75
Payment enclosed	$	_____

Please send a check or money order payable to Gold Eagle Books.

In the U.S.	In Canada
Gold Eagle Books	Gold Eagle Books
901 Fuhrmann Blvd.	P.O. Box 609
Box 1325	Fort Erie, Ontario
Buffalo, NY 14269-1325	L2A 5X3

Please Print

Name: _____

Address: _____

City: _____

State/Prov: _____

Zip/Postal Code: _____

SV:GZ-A